W

Coldsmith, Don
Thurnderstick

W

Coldsmith, Don
Thurnderstick

DATE	ISSUED TO
JUL 1 2 1993	87-460
JUL 2 1 1993	80-194
JUL 2 7 1993	91-67
AUG 0 01993	77-228
AUG 3 0 1993	77-148
SEP 1 4 1993	

Thunderstick

Also by Don Coldsmith

Thunderstick

»» »» »» »» »» »» »» »» »» »» »» »

DON COLDSMITH

A Double D Western
Doubleday

NEW YORK   LONDON   TORONTO   SYDNEY   AUCKLAND

A Double D Western
PUBLISHED BY DOUBLEDAY
a division of Bantam Doubleday Dell Publishing Group, Inc.
1540 Broadway, New York, New York 10036

Double D Western, Doubleday,
and the portrayal of the letters DD
are trademarks of Doubleday, a division of
Bantam Doubleday Dell Publishing Group, Inc.

Library of Congress Cataloging-in-Publication Data

Coldsmith, Don, 1926–
Thunderstick/Don Coldsmith.—1st ed.
p.   cm.—(A Double D western)
1. Indians of North America—Fiction.   I. Title.
PS3553.0445T48   1993
813'.54—dc20   92-39707
CIP

ISBN 0-385-47026-6
June 1993
First Edition

10   9   8   7   6   5   4   3   2   1

To the blackpowder shooter, whose first shot must count, because his thunderstick has only one.

Thunderstick

1
>> >> >>

In the history of the People, as recounted around the story fires, there was a pattern. Each time the nation encountered trouble with others with whom they came in contact, their reaction was the same. When it was over, they had a tendency to withdraw, to return to the old ways.

Is it not always so? Does the past not always seem safer, more secure than the present? And far more sure than the future.

The People had withdrawn in this way through the generations, because the old ways seemed safe. It was not that they were reluctant to try new ways. Were they not among the first on the plains to use the horse for hunting buffalo? It was because of that expertise that others called them the People of the Horse, or Elk-dog People.

They had been among the first to trade with the Spanish in Santa Fe for metal knives and lance points. They had guided the other outsiders when they came from the Northeast, the French, with their light-colored eyes and dark curls, who built towns along the River of the Kenzas and established a military presence. That was short-lived.

There is little doubt that their early use of the horse enabled the People to be in contact with these developments. Their mobility was also responsible for much of their own exploration. Their traditional territory reached from the mountains on the west to the woodlands east of the River of Swans, and from the Platte on the north to the oak-covered hills south of the Ar-kenzas River.

Their natural curiosity led them to travel and exploration in other areas. Consequently, into dangers not found in their own country. The tales told by the survivors of the exploring party that went "too far south" were horrible to relate.

Each time, then, that some of their probing contacts with others resulted in tragedy, the People reacted in the same manner: withdrawal to the privacy and security of the old ways. The familiarity of the songs and stories and rituals gave comfort, shutting out the newness that threatened.

Even so, their old ways were being changed, almost imperceptibly. It was easy to overlook the fact that many families now kindled their lodge fires with flint and steel instead of with yucca fire-sticks. Most lodges had a blanket or two, obtained in trade, in addition to the heavier buffalo robes. Many of the decorations that adorned shirts, dresses, and moccasins were now of glass or metal

beads and dangles, instead of the dyed quills of the porcupine.

It seems odd, then, that they were slow to adopt the
use of firearms for hunting and for war. They were not
unfamiliar to the People. Many had seen the thundersticks of the French, in their various contacts. There was
even a weapon or two in the possession of the People.

Old Dog Tooth, in the Red Rocks band, had a rusty,
inoperable musket that he had found in the southern
mountains. It was thought to be Spanish, and he kept it as
a memento, a curiosity. It made good conversation during
the social smokes of the winter moons.

Someone in the Eastern band was said to have part of a
broken French musket. But it seems likely that until now
no one had tried to learn the medicine of the thundersticks or how they could be useful to the People. Possibly
it was due to the fact that every contact with people who
used them had been unpleasant in some way. Not because of the thundersticks, necessarily. True, one of the
young men had been shot and nearly killed two generations ago in Santa Fe. But that was a misunderstanding, it
turned out later. There were no hard feelings.

The main reason for the slow adoption of this useful
tool must have been simply the reluctance to change the
old ways. The thunderstick required an entirely new way
of thinking, a new medicine, which seemed unnatural,
strange, and different.

Ultimately, of course, its usefulness became apparent,
along with the necessity for knowing more of the new
medicine involved in the care and use of the thunderstick.

• • • •

It was at the time of the Fall Hunt. Several young men of the Eastern band were spending time with the Southern band, socializing and participating in the hunt. There was good reason for this. The Southern band had not quite recovered from the loss of several of its finest young men on the disastrous expedition to the southern sea. This meant fewer men in proportion to the young women. Consequently, more girls were available for wives. There were young men of the other bands, searching or merely curious, attracted by this imbalance. "Like flies," one old woman snorted indignantly.

But it was a useful process. The young men who married into the band would probably remain with the wife's people, bringing the band back up to fighting strength and, at the very least, helping with the hunting while they were there. So they were largely welcomed.

True, there was some uneasiness that this fall, most of the temporary guests were from the Eastern band. That was mostly because of the area selected for the Southern band's summer camp. It was a bit farther east and north than usual, near the River of Swans, bordering closely on the range of the Eastern band.

But the uneasiness, it must be admitted, was primarily an ethnic tradition. To the rest of the tribe, the Eastern band had a reputation for foolishness. No one could remember how it had started originally, that demeaning slur on their status. It had been acquired sometime in the forgotten past and was now the source of jokes and stories which poked fun at the Eastern band. Any accident, any foolish mistake in the entire nation, might be noted with a remark that repeated the long-standing joke: *Aiee,* I did not know you were from the Eastern band!

It was a cruel joke, but there were always those who perpetuated it. Some, even, of the Eastern band, kept the joke alive by behaving foolishly, as if it were expected of them. That approach was a thorn in the flesh of the more capable leaders of the band.

"Do not act so," they advised indignantly. "That tells them they are right, that we *are* a foolish people."

It had gone on in this manner for many generations, despite the capable leaders who had arisen in that band. So now there were mixed feelings toward the three who were spending the summer with the proud Southern band, the first to possess and use the horse. Basically there was tolerance. These were bright, capable young men, and only occasionally was there a slighting remark, quietly and in private: "But would you want your daughter to marry one of them?"

This was not entirely lost on the young Eastern men. They were trying hard to overcome such preconceived notions.

"Prove yourself first," one of their wise Eastern chiefs had advised generations ago. "*Then* demand respect."

And it seemed that these young men were determined to do so. They were helpful and considerate, and their tentative gestures at courtship were reasonable and legitimate. Already there was one budding romance, and the sound of the courting flute was heard outside the lodge of the girl's parents.

"Well, let us see how they take part in the Fall Hunt," said one old woman, still skeptical. She would have to be convinced.

And now the time drew near. The wolves reported from their scouting forays that the great herds were on the move. It was time. Already long lines of geese had honked their way south, and the buffalo were moving also. The grass is always better just south of the coming of autumn, is it not? So preparations were under way for the great hunt which would provide each lodge with the winter's food supply. Now it would become evident whether the romantic young swains of the Eastern band were hunters or merely talkers and players of the song-flute.

Throughout the camp, men were busy putting finishing touches on their weapons. New arrows were feathered and painted, and the shafts straightened carefully over the fire. Bowstrings were replaced, and there were games and races to condition the horses. Some horse trading, too.

"Does he run right or left?"

"How do you want him to run?"

This factor was important, depending on the favorite weapon of the hunter. A hunter using the lance must approach the running buffalo from the left to allow for the thrust. A bowman, by contrast, must *shoot* to his left, because the bow is held in the left hand. Therefore, the approach is from the right of the animal. The preference of the horse becomes important in the confusion of the running herd.

Two of the visitors, it seemed, would use the bow, the third, a lance. They were not particularly interested in trading horses, having other things on their minds. But such things as horses and the hunt do have a tendency to come up in conversation with other young men. That was how it was known, their preference of weapons.

There was one curious thing, however. The answer of White Feathers, one of the Eastern men, seemed to make no sense. When asked about his horse, White Feathers had remarked quite casually that the animal ran "mostly to the right."

There was a ripple of gentle laughter. *Mostly?* There was a large unanswered question here. Was the horse poorly trained? The old doubts about the Eastern band and their traditional foolishness began to resurface. Was White Feathers so inept that he did not *know* his horse? That seemed unlikely. It was a fine-looking animal, and seemed responsive and well-trained. No one had seen the young man in a hunting situation, of course, but he had gone out with the scouts a time or two. They reported that he seemed quite capable, a good wolf and a good horse-man.

"Well, we will see!" exclaimed the old woman who was the keeper of most of the doubts.

She had a special interest in the strangers, because her granddaughter, in the bloom of young womanhood, was among the eligible.

"The Fall Hunt," she continued, "will separate men from boys!"

That very day, the wolves reported the herds near enough to begin specific plans. There would be a council tonight, with preparatory ritual dances.

2

》》》

Singing Wolf watched all these preparations with a new thrill. It would be his first big hunt, the first time he would ride in the chase. His horse was ready, he had checked his bow and each arrow many times.

Wolf already had kills to his credit, of course. A young cow elk . . . that had been a great feat, a fat yearling, almost as sweet as buffalo. Deer, of course, his first large game, and rabbits and squirrels before that, as he came up through the instruction of the Rabbit Society.

But now he was to become a hunter in this, his seventeenth summer. The leaders of the Elk-dog Society, his choice of the warrior fraternities, had given approval for him to participate. Then he would be eligible for membership and full initiation rites. It would also mark the coming of manhood. If his participation in the great Fall Hunt was deemed a success, it would open new vistas for him. With membership in the warrior society, he could, if he chose, speak in council. He did not know what he might want to say, but the right would be there, if he chose.

Probably the most important right that would come with the advance to manhood was more private, however. He would be eligible to marry. For many seasons he had looked forward to that. Not just a marriage, but a union with his lifelong friend, Rain. Her full name was seldom used. It was meant to commemorate the break in the blistering heat of the Red Moon . . . a special rain that breaks the drought, brings promise of a cooler autumn, and the return of green to the parched summer grasses. In the tongue of the People this drought-breaking rain was given a special word. In translation to the language of others, however, it became long and cumbersome. The Growers, with whom the People traded . . . Their allies, the Head Splitters . . . A simple, beautiful name became a liability. "Rain-That-Breaks-the-Drought-in-the-Red Moon . . ." *Aiee!* It was best to simply call her Rain, and so it was.

These two, Rain and young Singing Wolf, had grown up together, taken their instruction in the Rabbit Society, learned the songs and dances, the use of weapons, athletic skills, and the thrill of friendly competition. They had been one of those young couples who from childhood seemed destined to be together, to some day share a lodge. The adults of the Southern band had always assumed that when they were grown, these two would marry.

Wolf had always assumed so, too. That made it even more confusing when, this summer, the suitors from the Eastern band had arrived in the camp with their courting flutes and their sidelong glances. He watched with alarm as his friend Rain actually seemed to *enjoy* the advances of one of the strangers, a tall young man called White Feathers. This youth was perhaps a season or two older than Wolf, very handsome, and quite self-assured. Wolf found himself resenting the visitors, especially that one. He spoke to Rain about it.

"You should not encourage him."

The girl's dark eyes widened with surprise.

"Why not?" she demanded.

"Well . . . because . . . I thought . . . are *we* not to be together?"

Rain pretended surprise. "Oh, you thought *that?*" Her tone was sarcastic. "How is it you have not mentioned it?"

It was true. They had never talked of it. It had seemed unnecessary. Why speak of anything so obvious? This, of course, is a universal mistake, made by men everywhere. Confused and off balance, Singing Wolf tried to collect himself and give an answer.

"I . . . I . . . Rain, what are you talking about? You know I could not court you yet. I have not passed into a warrior society."

"But you could have said *something!*"

The situation was falling apart. Both were becoming angry, and both were stubborn young people. And neither, until this time, had ever been challenged to voice the feelings that were held for the other.

"I will listen to anyone's song that I choose!" Rain almost yelled at him. "You will not tell me what I must do or not do!"

Hurt and confused, Wolf retreated. Angrily, he took a step or two and then turned back to try to repair the hurt. But Rain was already walking away in long swinging strides. He loved to watch her walk . . . the shape of her legs, the swing of her hips and the sway of her graceful body . . . But now, the pleasure of watching her was gone. Those same curves and motions reflected only anger and determination.

How does a woman do that? he wondered. By the way she walks, a woman can say almost anything. She can express anger, disgust, flirtation, joy, indignation, seduction . . . Such expressive gifts are not given to mere men.

Wolf's anger rose as he watched her go. Anger at her, but more especially at the tall visitor. Yes, that was the cause of the quarrel. The stranger had no right to court *his* woman! Close on the heels of that thought came another, however. She was *not* his woman. She had plainly told him so, in words and actions. Jealousy burned . . . He thought of challenging the outsider to a fight. No, that would be ridiculous. In fantasy, he thought that maybe White Feathers would commit some heinous act which would permit Wolf to bring him to justice. It seemed unlikely, however. White Feathers appeared completely above reproach. The other two visitors seemed to follow his natural leadership abilities. Even Wolf had liked him, and had enjoyed talking with White Feathers and the other visitors. That had been before Wolf had realized the threat to his own relationship with Rain. *Aiee,* he thought, *this growing up is not as easy as it looks!*

He made his way back to the lodge of his parents and

sat down to lean against the willow backrest outside the door. His father was apparently not at home, so Wolf felt free to use the backrest. If his father returned, he would give up his seat, of course. Sometime, maybe he would make a backrest for himself. Not now . . . That was for older, more settled individuals. There were many things that he wished to do before he settled down. He had not even decided yet whether he wanted to follow his father's vocation as a medicine man of the People. There was time. So far, he was not even sure that he would be offered the gift of the spirit that such a responsibility required.

But now, all such speculation had been thrust aside by the threatened loss of his friend Rain. He sat, deeply preoccupied, staring at nothing, blankly lost in his own depressing thoughts.

Running Deer glanced out the lodge door.

"Ah, you are back!" she noted conversationally. "I hear the hunt will be tomorrow."

Her son nodded dully, disinterested. His enthusiasm was gone. This was not lost on his mother's keen sense of observation. She had always felt quite close to this, her youngest child.

"What is it, my son?" she asked, stepping through the doorway into the warm autumn sunlight.

"It is nothing, Mother."

Running Deer nodded. The opposite was apparent, of course, but she busied herself at the fire, building it up a little and placing some cooking stones in the flames to heat. Like his father, Wolf would talk when he was ready.

Singing Wolf was almost oblivious to his surroundings. He was dimly aware that his mother was carrying out routine tasks, but his mind was far away. He was thinking of the hunt now, and how he would prove himself, given the chance. Yes, he would prove his skill as a mighty hunter, better than the handsome visitor. He would demonstrate his bravery and his expertise, and the entire band would sing songs about Singing Wolf, the mighty killer of buffalo. With his help, the Southern band would have all the supplies they needed for the coming winter. He would be appreciated, and Rain would realize his importance to the People and to her. He could visualize the love in her eyes as she gazed into his face, enraptured. White Feathers would then slink away, his mission a failure, his leaving unnoticed in the excitement of the triumph of Singing Wolf.

Suddenly he realized that his mother had spoken.

"What is it, Mother?" he stammered as he came back to reality.

"I asked, is your horse ready?"

"What? Oh, yes." He tried to make it sound as if his heart was really in it, though the return to reality was a shock. He saw his mother's quizzical look and realized that she suspected something. He must gather his thoughts. "Yes, she is ready. I, too. It will be a great hunt."

He wished that he had been able to sound a little more logical. The answer he had just given sounded childish and . . . well, stupid! But his mother did not pry, and for that he was grateful.

"You are going to the dancing tonight?" she asked.

She knows that, he thought. *She is only trying to help.*

"Yes," he said aloud. "It will make everything ready."

Deer nodded. "Your father will be there, of course."

Still small talk.

"Where is he now?" asked Wolf.

"I do not know. He will be back soon, I think. We will all want to eat before we go to the ceremonies. Do you want to look for him, let him know that we will eat soon?"

Singing Wolf rose. It would give him something to do until other distractions provided relief from his depressing thoughts.

"It is good," he said.

"Do not be too long," his mother called after him.

He did not know exactly where to look. That was not his main purpose right now anyway, but his mission must appear reasonable. He turned toward an open area behind the camp. Here the young men frequently came to test their weapons. It was a shallow depression, perhaps two or three bow shots across. Not enough grass for a horse pasture, but open and pleasant, and close. Wolf had tried his new arrows there himself.

He had just topped the rise that overlooked the little valley when there was a muffled boom, like distant thunder. Quickly, Wolf glanced around the landscape. How had a storm approached unnoticed? He knew he had been distracted, but *aiee!* Yet he saw no clouds. Well, one puff of white, on the far side of the open space. It was so low that it touched the ground, though, and was now drifting downwind on the gentle breeze. Strange behavior for a cloud . . . Not layered out like a patch of fog. More like . . . ah, *smoke!* White smoke. But what . . . ?

There was a flurry of excitement over there, people running. Yet it did not seem to be in alarm, only interest. They were running *toward* the smoke-puff. Wolf trotted in that direction, listening to the excited shouts and peering ahead to try to determine the cause. He encountered his father, who was striding angrily back toward the camp, *away* from the excitement.

"Father! What is it?" Wolf demanded.

"Foolishness!" snapped the other. "One of those visitors from the Eastern band. He has a thunderstick, and he just fired it. Stupid! It may frighten the buffalo away and spoil the hunt!"

Singing Wolf had a special interest in this event now. "Which one?"

"Which one what?" asked Walks in the Sun.

"Which of the visitors?"

"Oh. That tall one, White Feathers, I think he is called. Foolish!"

The holy man turned and continued his way toward the camp. Wolf stood there a moment, undecided. He felt like shouting for joy. The tall, handsome, mature, and probably capable hunter who wished to court Rain had made a mistake. He had done a foolish thing which would be known now to all the camp. Even to Rain.

Singing Wolf turned to hurry after his father, trying to control his joy. *Aiee,* life was good after all!

3
>> >> >>

Singing Wolf sat on his horse just below the crest of the ridge, waiting with the other hunters. He was tense, his palms sweating, and his mind was racing. At any moment now, the scouts would give the signal and the long line of riders would cross the ridge at a walk to begin the hunt. This was the day, and whatever happened, his world would never be quite the same.

His mare fidgeted nervously, and he spoke to her as he laid a hand on her neck to steady her. All the horses were tense, as nervous as the riders. Many of the animals were experienced buffalo runners, veterans of many seasons. So, too, were some of the riders. To Wolf's left was a wiry old hunter, Three-legged Dog, who seemed almost bored at the wait. He held a lance across the withers of his horse, and there was something about his entire appearance which said that his reputation was well-earned. The man glanced around and their eyes met. There was no change in the old warrior's expression, only a slight nod of greeting. Wolf hoped that he could do well in the hunt, to earn a certain amount of respect from such a man as this. It was an honor even to ride with such a veteran.

To the right of Singing Wolf was Lone Beaver, a young man his own age. Beaver grinned at him, obviously as nervous as his friend. It was his first hunt also. Wolf gave him the hand sign for good luck.

The morning was chilly, the wet dew heavy on the grass. It had been a good growing season, the stalks thick and their seed heads ripe. The various grasses were beginning to turn their respective colors in the splendid show of autumn. The tallest of the real-grass and the golden plume-grass was as high as his horse. It was Wolf's favorite season, and his mind drifted to the observation of some of its pleasures. High overhead, a long line of geese traveled south, their cries heard only faintly in the distance. He could see the bright sunlight on their snowy wings, though the rays had not yet reached the slope where the hunters waited.

He heard the alarm cry of a crow and turned his glance in that direction. Along the crest of the ridge flew an owl, soft and quiet in its every motion. It was only above the tall grasses by a few hand-spans. In hot pursuit were two crows, diving and screaming at the silent hunting owl in the old ritual of harassment that had been going on since Creation. He smiled to himself, remembering the words of the little childhood song:

> *You hunted too long, Kookooskoos;*
> *day has come and your lodge is still far away.*

He wondered what his father would say about this. A favorable sign for the hunt, or not? He must ask later, maybe.

There was a movement now along the line of waiting hunters, as word was passed along to be ready. The herd must be approaching. Wolf shifted his grip on the bow and nervously fingered the reins. It was growing rapidly lighter now. The timing would be good.

Ah, now! Wolf suddenly knew that the buffalo were coming. It was possible that he heard the distant mutter of the herd, the lowing of the cows and the soft bleat of calves searching for their mothers. Maybe he had caught the heavy herd scent of countless warm furry bodies. Mostly, though, it was a sensation that he could not have explained. He could *feel* the presence, the spirits of a multitude of the great beasts, calmly grazing their way through the tallgrass prairie.

The horses felt it too, now. The nervous fidgeting increased. Perhaps they caught the scent, as the hidden hunting party was placed carefully downwind. As near as possible, of course, in the stillness of a quiet morning with its shifting breezes.

Now in the growing light, he noticed something he had not seen before. Beyond his friend Beaver was one of the visitors from the Eastern band, and beyond him, another. Yes, White Feathers. A wave of anger and resentment washed over him. Not the depression that he had felt before. That had lifted with the events of the past day. The handsome visitor had been severely reprimanded by the council last night for firing his musket. The entire Fall Hunt had been threatened by that unwise action. When the tongue-lashing by the band chieftain was over, there was no doubt in anyone's mind.

White Feathers had made a public apology for his thoughtlessness. He had handled that so well that even in his disgrace the young man seemed to gain prestige and respect. Not in the eyes of Singing Wolf, of course. There was no way that Wolf could see anything in this man that was worthy of respect. He understood why, of course, but it made no difference. His stomach churned, and there was a bitter taste in his mouth as he felt the rise of resentment, anger, and jealousy. Hate, even. How could Rain be attracted to such a despicable character, one so stupid as to fire his thunderstick before the hunt? And there the man sat, cool and confident, his weapon across his horse's withers.

Wolf wondered how many hunts White Feathers had had. Surely this was not his first. Had he used the thunderstick in a hunt, or was that new to him? Wolf studied the weapon as well as he could from this distance and without being too obvious. It was long and straight, except that a couple of hands' spans from one end it was crooked slightly. There was an irregularity about it at that point, too. Something tied to it or sticking out of it . . . he could not tell which. That end of the weapon, too, was broadened and flat, much like a canoe paddle. He wondered if it could also be used for that purpose. That would be handy.

It was also a puzzle how the thing worked. It was known that there must be small round stones, or balls of soft metal which formed a projectile. He did not see how a tiny thrown rock could do enough damage to take seriously. It must be the spell or magic, the medicine that was imparted to it. That was done, it was said, with a black substance, coarse like sand, which was poured into the hollow stick. It was probably the source of the power and magic. But how was it made to happen?

Wolf's thoughts returned to the real world as the line began to move forward. There was no longer any time to wonder about the medicine of the thunderstick.

The advance was at a walk, so as not to alarm the calmly grazing buffalo. They would start to run, of course, but the closer the hunters could approach before panic scattered the herd, the better. A long chase was hard on men and horses, and would result in fewer kills, fewer supplies for the coming winter.

The line of riders topped the hill, and now Wolf could see the hundreds of dark creatures, scattered as far as eye could see. The scouts had done well, carefully maneuvering a hundred or so of the animals into the meadow before them, separating them from the main herd. If possible, the experienced hunters at the mouth of this meadow would try to turn the leaders of the retreating smaller herd, creating a circular pattern. The other riders would then attempt to turn the frantically running animals back as they tried to break out into the open prairie to rejoin the main herd. If everything worked well, they could continue to shoot and spear until men and horses were exhausted or their quarry succeeded in breaking away.

Singing Wolf was fortunate, in that his position on the slope enabled him to see all this develop. At first, the grazing herd did not react at all to their approach. Then a wary old cow raised her head, sniffing the air suspiciously. A slight shift in the breeze? She trotted a few steps toward the advancing line, still testing the wind. Her limited vision did not yet identify the approaching figures as a danger. But her nose did. She wheeled to run, followed by her half-grown calf. Others sensed their alarm and in the space of a few heartbeats this entire segment of the herd was running, striving toward the open prairie. Close behind came the riders, beginning to shoot now when opportunity offered. Wolf saw a young bull go down from a lance thrust. He drew alongside a yearling cow and loosed an arrow, but another animal pushed in between. He could not tell whether his shot was effective.

The advance had been planned to partially encircle the herd from the left. Now hidden riders dashed out at the leaders, trying to turn them back to the right, to produce the circling effect. A couple of animals broke away and dashed for the timber along the creek, but mainly the maneuver was successful. Circling, yelling, shooting, pursuing an individual here and there, the riders settled into the edge of the circular pattern. Wolf heard a boom like thunder behind him and realized that White Feathers must have fired his weapon. Buffalo were stumbling, falling. Dust rose, obscuring the vision, in a confused melee of circling animals and riders.

Wolf had made one complete circuit, and had loosed two more arrows, when his horse drew alongside a fat cow. The approach was from the right, which placed him inside the outer fringes of the circle. He drew the arrow to its head and released it . . . Ah! a good hit! But before the stricken cow even stumbled, Wolf felt his mare shy away from something on her right. He had been concentrating only on his quarry and had neglected to watch there.

A huge bull had pulled out of the circling melee and had charged one of his tormentors. At least, the bull seemed to interpret it so. Wolf caught barely a glimpse of the massive head before it was thrust under him. The shiny horns swung, piercing the soft underbelly of the gray mare. She screamed with pain and terror as she was lifted high and tossed. Singing Wolf, lifted even higher, found himself for one dreadful moment above the dusty scene. It seemed that time stood still as he looked down on the back of the great bull. An arrow jutted from its flank, tormenting it even more than the chase. Oddly, his attention fixed on that feathered shaft as the world stopped for a moment. *And it is not even my arrow,* he thought. Beyond lay the stricken mare, her last dying struggles pushing ropy white loops of intestine out into the grass.

Then he began to fall. He struck squarely on the back of the furious bull, bouncing away as the animal whirled. Wolf had long since dropped his weapons, though they would have done no good now. The bull turned, its little eyes searching. The arrow wound might eventually prove fatal, but just now was merely a source of pain and anger. The eyes fastened on Wolf's helpless form as he lay gasping for breath. He could not have moved if it meant his life, which for all practical purposes it did. Numbly, he saw the creature paw up a clod of turf with a forefoot, tossing it high. The head lowered, and Wolf prepared to face death on the shining black tips of the bull's horns. He wanted to close his eyes but could not.

Then, with a roar of thunder, a miracle seemed to take place. The raging bull stopped, shuddered, and threw up its head, to fall stiffly to one side. There it lay, the eyes glazing, while the hind legs kicked feebly.

The main portion of the milling circle had moved on, and the thunder of hooves was quieting. A horseman appeared, ghostlike in the cloudy pall of dust. Wolf recognized White Feathers, who now swung down and approached the fallen hunter.

"Are you hurt?" he asked.

"I do not know. I hurt everywhere, but I am alive, I think."

"It is good."

Wolf was recovering his breath now, and his thoughts were whirling. The past two days had been extremely difficult for him. It took a moment to realize what had just happened. He had been unhorsed, his mare killed by the wounded bull, and the bull had then turned in mad rage to finish her fallen rider. But something had prevented . . . the bull had fallen dead . . . that sound of thunder! *Aiee!* White Feathers must have killed it with his thunderstick!

This thought, perhaps, was the most difficult of all to accept. He had liked and admired this young visitor, until he realized that White Feathers wished to court Rain. Then Wolf had disliked everything about him. His handsome looks, his leadership, his popularity, the way Rain looked at him. Wolf had rejoiced over the foolish mistake that brought a reprimand to White Feathers. One should not take pleasure in the misfortunes of others, but this was a special case. It gave Singing Wolf a new start. He had entered the hunt with a determination to make a better showing than White Feathers. Instead, he had lost his horse, had nearly been killed himself, and that was not the worst.

The worst was that his life had been saved by the rival that he hated. The hero of the great Fall Hunt was White Feathers.

4

≫ ≫ ≫

There was long and sometimes heated discussion the next night at the council. Normally there would not even have been a council so close on the heels of a hunt. There was too much to do, dressing out and butchering, slicing meat and hanging it to dry. Everyone became involved, even small children. They could assist by guarding the family's drying meat, shooing away flies and the occasional crow that became overly bold.

Yet even as the work went on, there was a constant chatter of discussion about the hunt. There was always the retelling of feats of skill and daring, laughter at misfortune, and tales of the one that got away. This time, however, there was a special impact to one misfortune. A horse had been gored, tossed and killed. That had hap-

pened before, though not for a while. The rider of the
dead mare had earned a reputation as a hunter. His skill
was not in question, for three of the kills that lay strewn
across the valley had been impaled by the arrows of young
Singing Wolf. His prestige was soaring, for he had done
well on his first hunt.

Even that was overshadowed, however, by the circumstances. The story had been told and retold. The unhorsed Wolf, helpless under the charge of the wounded
bull, would now be dead, except . . . The real hero of
the day was White Feathers, the visitor from the Eastern
band. That one had fearlessly faced the great bull and
struck it down with one shot from his thunderstick. Feathers had been in disrepute before, over his unwise use of
that weapon. That was gone now. His heroic act and his
skill with the outlandish weapon had saved the life of
Singing Wolf.

Wolf himself was glum. He was stiff and sore in every
muscle, still finding new hurts each time he moved. Even
that was not as great as the quiet jibes by some of his
friends.

"How does it feel, Wolf," his friend Fast Turtle asked in
mock seriousness, "to be saved by one of the Eastern
band?"

Even that, however, was only an annoyance compared
to the real hurt. That was an unspoken thing, but one that
cut deeply, driving a pain through his heart that would not
go away. It was the expression in the eyes of Rain when
she looked at the visitor from the Eastern band. A look of
sheer adoration, which tore at the vitals of young Wolf.

He tried to avoid her, with some degree of success, but
he knew that there was no way that he could do so over a

long time. She *had* smiled at him, even placed a hand on his arm, and told him that she was glad he had not been killed. But that, he thought, was merely out of pity, and made the hurt deeper.

Wolf dreaded the council, because he knew that the events around his hunt would be discussed and his hated rival publicly praised. But he could not fail to attend. It would be impolite, because Wolf, too, would be honored. Also, not to be present would dishonor the man who had saved his life. *Aiee*, he had not realized how complicated it is to grow up!

The pipe was lighted, circulated, the fragrant smoke offered to the appropriate winds and spirits, and was now returned to its case. Broken Lance, the old band chieftain, handed the instrument to his pipe bearer and began the council.

"My brothers, it has been a good hunt. But there are things of which we must talk."

The story of the hunt and its uncommon features was then retold. Wolf was embarrassed at the attention, even though it was all favorable. Then came the most distasteful part, the praise of his rival, White Feathers. It was disgusting, thought Wolf, to see men who had been the most critical of the visitor two days ago now praising him. If one more man recounted the bravery and skill of White Feathers, he thought, it would be too much to endure.

Finally, though, the praise was over, and the chief turned to White Feathers.

"My brother," he said, "please tell us of the thunderstick which you used so well. Some of us have seen them sometimes, but we know little of this weapon."

Aiee, thought Wolf, *this is the worst yet*.

White Feathers rose, calm and confident, still making a good impression with his modest manner. He showed his weapon, told of its power and distance, and then offered to demonstrate its use.

"But it is dark," protested someone.

White Feathers nodded. "True," he agreed. "We cannot see where the shot strikes, but we do not need to. We do not try to recover the ball, as we would an arrow."

"Is that not wasteful?"

"No . . . maybe a little, but the ball can be replaced easily."

White Feathers answered every question smoothly and easily.

"What about the black sand that contains the medicine?" a man asked.

"It is in this horn," Feathers answered. "See?"

He removed the wooden stopper from the buffalo horn that hung around his neck and sprinkled a few grains into his palm.

"Now, watch!"

He stepped toward the fire and tossed the powder into the flames. There was a flash of light, a soft *pouf,* and a cloud of cottony smoke arose. Some of those on the front row scrambled backward, crablike, retreating from the unknown.

"It takes fire to do that?" asked the chief.

"Yes, Uncle. The fire is supplied by this flint, fastened in the jaws here. It strikes the metal to make a spark, just as we do to build our fires."

There was a mutter, acknowledging the fact that some still disapproved of such a fire-starter. The more conservative still preferred the traditional fire-sticks.

But there were yet other objections.

"A man in the Red Rocks band has one of these," stated an old man. "It is useless, except to look and wonder about."

White Feathers nodded.

"I do not know this man," he said, "but if he does not understand its use, of course it is useless. Where did he get the thunderstick?"

The old man shrugged. "He found it, maybe. I do not know."

White Feathers nodded again. "Of course. It is important to learn the use of its medicine. He must have that skill."

Another, a younger man, rose.

"My brother, if I have lost or used all my arrows, I can make more. What if all your medicine is used up?"

"I must plan ahead, get more of the powder and lead before I need it. Do you not do that with arrows?"

There was general laughter.

"May we see this weapon shoot, in the air?" someone asked.

White Feathers turned to the chief, who nodded permission.

"There is already the medicine powder inside," he explained. "I have pushed the ball down on top of it. Now, I put a little powder under this lid"—he lifted the frizzen to sprinkle powder in the pan—"and close it. Then, when I am ready to shoot, I pull the flint back and push this little stick to . . ."

His last word or two was lost in the sound of the gun. Those nearest could see the flint fall, pushing the steel frizzen forward from its position covering the powder.

There was only a fraction of an instant before the sparks struck the powder with a flash and smoke and dull *pouf.* Closely following came the boom of the main charge. The weapon bucked, fire belched from the muzzle, and dense, cottony smoke rose in a cloud that obscured White Feathers for a moment. Then he lowered the weapon, as excited talk erupted. He began to reload.

"What if it rains?" someone asked. "Would your fire start?"

There was general laughter.

"The medicine powder must be kept dry," White Feathers admitted. "That is why it is kept tightly closed in this horn."

The next question was along a different line.

"How far will it shoot?"

"Farther than an arrow, and as straight."

"But I can use my arrow again!"

"True, but . . ."

"Enough!" Broken Lance raised a hand. "Let us not argue. I am made to think that there are things that are good and bad. White Feathers, do many of your people have this thunderstick?"

"Only a few, Uncle. But more are interested."

"And where would one get such a thing?"

"From the French. They have set up trading places, more than before. They want furs."

The chief nodded thoughtfully. He had seen many winters, many new things and new leaders come and go. His knowledge seemed ageless.

"We used to trade in Santa Fe, but not for thundersticks. A generation ago, maybe."

"Yes," White Feathers agreed. "It is much the same. But closer. Soon everyone will have thundersticks."

Broken Lance was still thoughtful, quiet. No one else spoke and finally he nodded again. "That," he observed, "is what concerns me."

Now discussion erupted, excited and active. Opinions quickly separated into two, those who coveted thundersticks for immediate use and those who were reluctant.

"How could you prepare to shoot again while on a horse?" someone called. There was laughter.

"It is a little slower," admitted White Feathers, "but possible. And you can shoot from either side!"

An unspoken undercurrent was a vague uneasiness that was hard to admit. Namely, what if all of the Eastern band obtain thundersticks and we have none, and they turn out to be *good?* It would appear very uncomplimentary to be more backward than the Eastern band. Undoubtedly Broken Lance was thinking of this, among other considerations. Finally he lifted a hand for quiet.

"I am made to think," he said, "that we must learn more of this. What if we have trouble again with the Shaved-heads of the forest to the east? What if *they* have this weapon, and we do not?"

Apparently few had considered this. Broken Lance continued after a moment's pause for effect.

"Now, you say the French want furs in trade?"

"Yes, Uncle."

"Of course furs are not yet thick and soft this season. But let us keep this in mind as we winter. We can have furs to trade by spring. Then we can send a party to trade."

There were nods of agreement, and the chief continued.

"Now, we have two men with great experience. I wish
to ask them of this. Walks in the Sun, on the great journey
south, did your party see these thundersticks in use?"

"No, my chief. The Spanish use them, but we did not
see any."

The chief turned now to another.

"Strong Bow, when you were with your wife's people
on the Platte, did they use this weapon?"

"A few, my chief. They trade a little with the French.
But I have no personal knowledge."

"Yes, it is as we thought. But, my brothers, this is all
around us. We must not be the last to obtain this thunderstick. I am made to think that it may be as important as
when we got the horse."

This was a big statement, one which showed that the
old chief had considered this step for a long time. He
went on.

"Strong Bow, would you and Walks in the Sun lead a
trading party in the spring? I am sure that our young
brother here," he indicated White Feathers, "will guide
your party to this trading place of the Sky-eyes."

Singing Wolf's heart sank. His rival was even more of a
hero now and had just been invited by the chief to spend
the winter with the Southern band. At least, Broken
Lance's last remark seemed to imply such an invitation. It
would be a hard winter for Singing Wolf.

5

>> >> >>

It *was* a hard winter. Cold Maker swept down from his home in the northern mountains, attacking again and again. Sun Boy seemed for a while to have lost heart. There were times when he did not show himself for many days. Even when he did, there were those who privately worried that his torch was too far gone to renew. It cast a pale yellow light, sickly and weak, across drifting snow that told of Cold Maker's power.

"We should have wintered farther south," an old woman complained.

"But not too far!" her friend answered.

"Of course not. But I have never liked it here. It is too dangerous."

That much was true. They were on the edge of country

claimed by the Shaved-head forest people. There had been disastrous contacts before. But Broken Lance, in the wisdom of his many winters, had chosen this site. It was believed that the Shaved-heads would not attack so large and strong a camp as that of the Southern band. It seemed an accurate assumption. The wolves of the People had found evidence that they were being watched, but there was no overt activity. Probably the hard winter and deep snow had been helpful, too. Such a winter is no time to send out a war party. The Shaved-heads would know that.

Unfortunately, such a winter was not the easiest in which to trap furs, either. There was risk even in running trap lines. A sudden change in the weather might leave a lone trapper stranded without shelter. To that unfortunate one, it would make little difference that the furs the People did manage to collect were thick and soft.

For Singing Wolf, the hard winter was good. With Cold Maker howling outside the lodges, there had been less socializing than usual. There were, of course, the paths of tramped-down snow that led from one lodge to another through the camp. The paths that led to the sheltered meadow where the horse herd was held were kept open. But it was the sort of bitter season when one would avoid going out if at all possible. Each lodge had been stuffed with dry grass between the outer cover and the lodge lining. In addition, the drifting snow, piled high around the lodges, furnished more protection.

"Cold Maker has outsmarted himself," chuckled the old people. "His snow helps more than it hurts."

That was true, as long as the supplies of each lodge, and the available fuel, held out. Both of those commodities were available in good quantity. The good Fall Hunt had been a fortunate thing.

So, despite the hard season, the People had wintered well. It was a fact, though, that there had been less socializing. Some, of course. On a day when the bitter wind was calm as Cold Maker paused to regather his strength, a man would often stand before his lodge to offer an invitation.

"Ah-koh, my friends, come and smoke!" he would call.

And there were always those who came, eager for conversation, smoking, and maybe a little gambling with the plum stones. But this was certainly not as social a season as most. After all, one who braved the cutting edge of Cold Maker's wind to join the event must do so again when it was time to go home.

For this entire lessening of social activity, Singing Wolf was grateful. Though it made it more difficult to trap, it also kept White Feathers from being out as actively. Consequently there was less contact between the visitor and the young woman who had been Wolf's friend for as long as he could remember. That was now a very uncomfortable situation. He would have liked to go to her, to talk out their misunderstanding, but his pride would not let him. In addition, there was now the danger that she would only laugh at him and turn him away. That embarrassment he dared not risk, because it might mean losing her forever. If indeed, he thought glumly, he had not already lost her.

So it was very slim encouragement that the two could not spend much time together. But it was all that he had. He put himself wholeheartedly into his trapping, trying to forget the major threat in his life. It was not successful in that respect, but it did help to increase the pile of prime furs that grew in Wolf's part of the lodge of his parents.

He began to talk to older men who had experience in such things. He devised deadfalls and snares with sensitive triggers, using his own ideas as well as the instruction of the old men.

Eventually, Sun Boy began his counterattack, armed with a renewed torch and a gentle south wind. By this time, Singing Wolf had begun to achieve a reputation for his skill as a trapper. He did not care, much. That was not the purpose. But it is good to be admired.

He was not prepared, however, when White Feathers approached him with words of praise.

"It is said that you have done well with the furs," stated the visitor. "It is good. I will help you with the trading."

Wolf's head swam for a moment. The unexpected remark was confusing enough in itself. Even though such a compliment was to be desired, this one was unacceptable. He did not want favors from anyone, especially this man. It was all he could do to remain calm.

"Thank you," he said modestly. "I have been fortunate."

White Feathers shook his head.

"It is more than that," he insisted. "You are skilled."

Wolf did not know what to say. It is perhaps the most difficult thing to do, to accept praise from someone we dislike. We would like to believe that a rival's judgment is poor, yet when he judges that *we* are skilled, it must be good. Wolf managed to gulp out a clumsy answer.

"I . . . I try . . ." he stammered.

White Feathers smiled, the beautiful friendly smile that made people like him instantly. He chuckled. "It is good!"

It was sometime later that Wolf had another thought.

Feathers had offered to help him with the trading. Yet he, Wolf, had no intention of going with the party that his father would lead. No, he would stay with his mother, looking after her until his father's return. He was rather looking forward to it. It would afford some time to be reacquainted with Rain . . . time without the complication of White Feathers' presence in the camp. Yes, it would be good.

But why, an elusive thought kept nagging, why did the visitor assume that Wolf would be there with the trading party? Maybe he was only offering to represent . . . ? No, that was not what White Feathers had said.

Wolf thought of all this as he was checking his traps. This would be the last time, he thought. The season was over, and the warm days would quickly thin the fur. In fact, Wolf was removing the snares that were still set, letting deadfalls tumble down. The take was small today, anyway.

He was just removing a mink from beneath the log of one of the deadfalls when something made him look up. There stood a young man of about his own age, no more than a stone's throw away. The other was dressed in breechclout and leggings, and a loose shirt of buckskin. His head was shaved on the sides, leaving a roach of hair up the center of the head. In one hand he carried the limp form of an otter and in the other a thunderstick similar to that of White Feathers.

Wolf glanced around quickly, but saw no more Shaved-heads. His heart beat faster. How would the other react? These forest people were notoriously unpredictable. Would he attack? If so, the thunderstick was an unknown quantity. Wolf had laid his bow aside, but now decided to make a try to arm himself. With deliberate moves, though slowly, he reached to pick up the weapon, still watching the other man. It was a moment before the Shaved-head seemed to understand what he was doing. Then, to his horror, Wolf saw the muzzle of the thunderstick swing upward. He had not even fitted his arrow to the bowstring yet when the fire belched from the other's weapon, and the woods echoed with its boom.

Wolf had seen the flash in the priming pan and dropped flat behind the log of the deadfall. That would probably not have been enough to save him, but the other trapper's aim was not good anyway. Wolf saw and heard a piece of bark knocked from a nearby tree.

It was happening rapidly, but even so, the thought struck him that it would take the other man some time to reload his thunderstick. He had seen White Feathers do this and knew that he had a little time. The thought was hardly finished when he was up, hurdled the logs of the deadfall, and sprinted toward the enemy. He had left his bow behind, and drew his ax from his belt as he ran.

The melting snow was slippery; he had to be careful of his footing. He covered the distance between them quickly. The other man was struggling to pour powder from a horn, then one of the round lead balls. He fumbled and dropped several of the bullets in the snow. Wolf was not certain whether he had managed to put one into the weapon's muzzle or not, but it did not matter. He had not even begun to lift the lid of the priming pan when Wolf rushed upon him.

The Shaved-head looked up in alarm, took a step back, and his moccasin landed on a slippery spot of slush. Melt-

ing snow had dripped from the tree above and was col-
lecting in little rivulets. The man slipped and fell heavily,
rolled over and lifted a hand in futile defense against the
deadly blow of the ax.

Wolf saw the terror of death in the eyes of the young
man and paused for a moment. He could not strike. The
other was younger than he thought, a mere boy, now defenseless and helpless.

Wolf reached down and took the knife from the youth's
waist and picked up the thunderstick, watching carefully
and keeping the ax ready. The thunderstick was much
heavier than he had imagined. He stepped back and laid
the weapons out of reach. Then he shifted the ax to his
left hand and began to sign. First, the hand sign for peace,
right hand raised, palm forward. There was no reaction in
the burning dark eyes of the youth.

"How are you called?" Wolf signed.

"It does not matter. Kill me!"

That would have been the safest course, but now Wolf
had created a problem for himself. Once having looked
into the terror-stricken face, it would be very difficult. He
would have had no trouble if they had shot at each other
about the same time. He could even have killed the other
as he ran, Wolf thought, but not lying helpless here before
him.

"Get up," he motioned.

Cautiously the youth sat up.

"Far enough," Wolf signed. "Why did you try to shoot
me?"

"This is our country to trap," signed the youth angrily.

"But we are here only a little while. Soon we leave and
will not be back."

"Is this true?"

"Of course. Ours is the grassland. We only wintered here."

"My people knew you were here."

"Yes, I know. But now we leave. I do not want to kill you."

"You may as well. I am defeated."

"No, you slipped and fell. If I kill you, your people will come and try to kill us."

"That is true."

"I will let you go, to tell them we mean no harm here. We leave soon."

The young man brightened.

"Really?"

"I do this for myself, not for you," Wolf cautioned. "I do not want enemies following me. You can tell them."

"I can have my weapons?"

Wolf thought for a moment.

"Your knife. Your fur, too." He gestured toward the otter. "I keep the thunderstick."

There was a new look of alarm in the young man's face.

"It is my father's!"

"Maybe you should have thought of that."

"But . . ."

"You have your life," Wolf reminded him.

"That is true," the young man signed glumly. "Now, how are you called?"

"Why do you ask?"

"So I can tell my father who has his thunderstick."

Wolf laughed.

"Tell him who spared his son," he signed. "Singing Wolf, of the Elk-dog People. But tell him, too, that we are leaving, and that we mean no harm."

6
》》》

It must be admitted that the encounter of Singing Wolf with the young Shaved-head caused deep concern in the camp of the People.

"You should have killed him!" Fast Turtle insisted.

"But you were not there, Turtle. You do not know how it was."

"He tried to kill you!"

"Yes, but he did not. We talked, using hand signs. That made it harder."

"The hand signs?"

"No! It is harder to kill somebody if you have been talking to him. *Aiee*, Turtle, you must understand."

There were others who came much closer to understanding. Wolf had immediately gone to his father when he returned to the camp, and the two hurried to the lodge of the chief.

"My son has a thing to tell you," explained Walks in the Sun.

Old Broken Lance listened to the account without comment. When Wolf was finished he remained silent a little while, smoking thoughtfully. Finally the pipe seemed to go out, and the old man knocked the dottle into his palm and tossed it into the fire. He laid the pipe aside. It was not the ceremonial pipe, so required less formal attention.

"And this is the thunderstick he carried?" asked Broken Lance.

"Yes, Uncle. I thought I should keep it."

The old man examined the weapon curiously, turning it over in his hands.

"It is good. But it is also good that you did not kill him."

Singing Wolf felt exonerated. He had been in doubt about that, feeling that he had not measured up as a warrior of the People.

"Yes," continued the chief, "to kill him would have brought on an attack. But this does change things."

"How is that, Uncle?" asked Walks in the Sun.

"We cannot send the party to trade with the French now. It would weaken the rest of the band to send those warriors away. The Shaved-heads might decide to attack."

This seemed a logical risk. Wolf was disappointed, because it meant that White Feathers would be around a while longer. He had wintered in the lodge of the chief, whose children were grown and had lodges of their own. It had been apparent that Broken Lance and his wife rejoiced in the opportunity to have a young person in their lodge again.

At that moment the doorskin was drawn aside and White Feathers himself entered.

"*Ah-koh,* Uncle. You sent for me?"

"Yes, come in, my almost-son. We need your counsel."

Singing Wolf wished that he could find an excuse to leave. It was extremely distasteful to sit and see his rival in a situation where the band's leaders asked for advice. Now Broken Lance handed the thunderstick to White Feathers.

"This was taken from a Shaved-head by our brother here," he explained.

"*Aiee!* You killed him?"

"No. I let him go."

White Feathers made no comment but examined the weapon.

"It is loaded?" he asked.

"No. He shot it at me and missed."

"It is much like mine."

"French?" asked Walks in the Sun.

"Maybe so, Uncle. I have seen no other," said White Feathers respectfully. "It looks much like mine."

You said that already, thought Wolf. He was having a difficult time relating at all to this young man. And now, if the trading party was to be postponed . . . Spring coming, the time of romance, White Feathers and his courting flute still around . . . The thought was like ashes in his mouth.

"So," Broken Lance was saying, "it is as we feared. The Shaved-heads *do* have the thundersticks. My brothers, this is a dangerous situation."

The others nodded silently, waiting for the chief to continue. He seemed lost in thought for a long time, sitting quietly with bowed head. Wolf thought for a moment that he might have fallen asleep, as the old sometimes do. But, in a little while, Broken Lance raised his head. His eyes were quick and alert as he glanced from one to the other.

"My brothers," he said, "let us think on this and pray for guidance. And spread the word . . . a council, to-night."

Broken Lance had seen many winters, thought Wolf as he left the lodge, but his mind was as clear as a frosty morning. This man had been a leader before Wolf was born, and he was still a leader.

The People began to gather for the council well before dark. Word had spread that there would be major decisions tonight. Besides, everyone wanted to hear more of Singing Wolf's adventure with the Shaved-head. That story had already grown with the telling, even by those who had not even talked to Wolf himself.

The fire had been started. Nights were still uncomfortably cold, even in the Moon of Awakening. This fire was not large, because fuel was scarce after a cold winter. The council would be brief, much shorter than one where the ground on which they sat was warm instead of frozen. Winter councils, of course, could be held in the lodge of the chief, but attendance would be limited by space. This would be an open council, for all to attend, because it involved changing plans for the entire band.

The murmur of conversation quieted as Broken Lance performed the opening smoke ceremonies, which were deliberate but quickly completed. There was a complete hush as the chief started to speak.

"My brothers," he began, "I know you have all heard of the thing that has happened to our brother Singing Wolf."

There was a murmur around the circle, and the chief waited for it to settle.

"We need to send a party to trade furs and get thunder-sticks," he went on, "but it would divide our strength. Both that party and the camp would be in danger of attack. So I am made to think that we should change our plan."

The murmur was louder, as various ideas burst to the surface. Some of these were extreme . . . an attack on the Shaved-heads . . . a union with Eastern band for strength. But Broken Lance did not even let a discussion arise. He lifted a hand for silence.

"We will break camp in three days," he announced.

There was stunned silence for a moment, and then one of the respected warriors rose.

"My chief," he began, "will that not seem to be a retreat?"

Broken Lance looked at him keenly.

"Not if it is well ordered," he said. "We will move deliberately, slowly, ready to defend. The Shaved-heads have never followed us out onto the plains."

There were doubts, but not much resistance. It was apparent that it would be unwise to divide the band at this time. It also appeared good to leave the country of the Shaved-heads before the weather really opened up, allowing movement of major war parties.

The risks were known to all. A moving band is more vulnerable than one in a fixed location. They would have to be alert to any attack on the column. But two factors led to the general agreement. One was the age-old tradi-

tional right of the band chief to decide the time for a
move. It was seldom challenged.

The other was an even more nebulous thing, the call of
the open sky to the People. It was good to seek shelter for
winter camp, to have a fringe of timber to protect against
the howling winds of Cold Maker's repeated attacks. Even
so, it was always a great relief to break winter camp, move
back to the far horizons of the prairie, and stretch the
eyes again in the seeing of far distances. To be surrounded
by trees is, to children of the plains, to feel trapped and
enclosed, like a cornered animal, with no escape evident.

So it was probably this factor, deeply felt but difficult to
describe, that led to the general acceptance of a move.

"What if the weather turns bad?" asked someone.

That was certainly a possibility at this time of year. A
few warm days, the melting of snow and the few sprigs of
green that would appear were deceptive. Cold Maker
might easily make one last counterattack as he retreated.
Food for the horses would be unreliable for yet another
moon. Yes, it was risky. But no more dangerous, most
people thought, than staying here, waiting for an attack by
the Shaved-heads.

Broken Lance answered the question calmly and with
dignity, befitting his position.

"If the weather is bad," he stated, "we will stop and
camp."

So the People began to prepare for the move. There
was much to do, but it was not as if they were moving in
the autumn. Supplies were low at this time, making pack-
ing easier. The main thing was to make this move appear
deliberate, rather than a retreat in fear. Extra wolves were

sent out to circle the camp at all times, against the possibility of a surprise attack, but no threat was reported.

Broken Lance called Wolf back for another conversation.

"You told the Shaved-head that we were leaving?" he asked.

"Yes, Uncle. Was I wrong to do that?"

"No . . . no, I think maybe not. It makes our intention clear."

"That was my purpose, Uncle."

The old man nodded.

"Yes, it is good. It may be a help."

"How so, my chief?"

"Well, we could leave today. It could be done. But that would look like flight. If we take the usual three days, it appears unhurried. They know we intend to move, because you have said so. Then they see us do so, without hurry . . . They are watching us, of course."

With a quick hand sign, the chief signaled that the dialog was at an end. Singing Wolf rose and made his way around the fire toward the door. He was reaching for the doorskin when the voice of Broken Lance stopped him.

"Oh, yes, Wolf. Be careful about speaking for the People when you have no authority to do so."

Wolf nodded clumsily, embarrassed, and slipped outside. He stood there for a moment, his cheeks burning with shame. He had been honored to be called before the chief, and not until now had he realized that it was a reprimand. A gentle scolding, to be sure, but *aiee*, he should have known better.

Disgruntled, he left the camp to be alone and think for a little while. He must recover from the criticism. A walk over to the horse herd would seem logical, and he turned that way. He would have preferred even more solitude, but under the circumstances it would be too dangerous to be outside the camp.

Now, to his annoyance, he realized that someone was following him. Hurrying, even, to catch up, from the sound of the other's footsteps in the wet snow. He stopped and turned. It was White Feathers, probably the person he would rather *not* see just now over any in the world. But he could not avoid it. He waited while the young man approached.

Wolf glumly acknowledged the greeting, resenting the man, hating the cheerful smile. What could White Feathers want?

"I saw your thunderstick, that you took from the Shaved-head," began Feathers. "It is good."

Wolf nodded uncertainly.

"You took none of his bullets and powder?"

Singing Wolf had not even had time to think of that. *Aiee,* one more evidence of his stupidity. It was like having a bow but no arrows. He felt chastised again.

"No . . . I . . . he dropped them in the snow," he mumbled.

"Ah, yes! I wondered. But you will need some."

"Maybe so."

"Look . . . I have only a little powder and lead, but I will show you, help you learn to use your thunderstick. Then, when you go to trade, you can get more."

It was a generous offer. At the moment, Wolf did not want any help of any sort with anything. Especially help from this hated rival. He owed his life to this young man, which in itself was a thorn in the flesh. Now he must also accept instruction. It was almost intolerable. He tried to think, to remain calm, choking back the angry words that rose in his throat. He *needed* this help, this instruction.

"It is good," he managed to mumble through clenched teeth.

7

White Feathers rolled several of the shiny round balls from his pouch into the palm of his hand. He selected one and replaced the others, closing the drawstring.

"This is the ball, or bullet," he explained. "The medicine powder throws it like an arrow or a rock. Let us see if it fits your gun . . ."

It was a loose fit, rolling easily into the smooth tube.

"No matter," said White Feathers. "You can use a patch of thin buckskin or a piece of an old blanket. When we get to the traders you will need a bullet mold anyway."

There it goes again, thought Singing Wolf; *it is assumed that I will go with the trade party.* He really did not want to do so. To be in the company of White Feathers any longer than absolutely necessary was becoming more distasteful daily.

Even so, he *was* grateful for the information. Strange, how a person can like and admire many things about another, and at the same time dislike other things. It was good of White Feathers to help and advise him about the new weapon, and he did benefit from it. So it was appreciated.

"You will need a pouch to carry some of these things," White Feathers continued. "Balls, extra flints, some patches."

He opened the pouch that hung at his side. Inside were scraps of greasy cloth. White Feathers pulled one out and wrapped it around the bullet to try in the bore.

"No, too thin for this bullet. We will find something else. But this grease is important, Wolf. Tallow. It lets the bullet slide smooth and fast. Oh, yes, we should clean your gun. It was fired at you, you said?"

"Yes."

"Well, the spirits of the medicine powder leave bad thoughts behind. They begin to grow the red rust that eats metal."

"*Aiee!* Is this not dangerous?"

"Only to metal. I think it is like planting seeds, as the Growers do, but these grow only in metal."

"How is this stopped?"

"By washing them out before they take root. See this stick?" He drew the rod from beneath the barrel of the weapon. There was a slot near one end. "You put a wet bit of cloth in that hole to wipe out the black stain that begins to eat metal. Then grease it."

"*Aiee*, there is so much to learn!"

"Not so much, really. You will see. But now let us try your weapon. Here is how to measure the powder."

He placed the lead ball on his left palm and took the wooden peg from the mouth of his powder horn. Carefully, he began to trickle powder from the container, letting it fall on the surface of the ball and pour off into his palm.

"It should just cover the ball," he said, stopping when it did so. "Now, this much powder goes into the gun." He poured it as he spoke. "You will want to make a measure . . . a horn tip or a piece of an antler, maybe. Make a hole in it to measure the powder."

"But how did you do that on a horse, on the buffalo hunt?"

"I didn't. In a hurry, or if you have to, you can just pour from the horn and guess. It does not shoot as straight, but makes the next shot quicker."

Wolf did not know how he was going to absorb all of this information, but he would try. He must eventually be at least as skillful with this weapon as White Feathers. Otherwise, he thought, he had no chance with Rain. He had not seen her much in all the hurry of preparation to break camp. That would take place tomorrow, and White Feathers had thought it advisable that Wolf learn about the new thunderstick before the move began. It was good in more than one way, thought Wolf. While the visitor was with Wolf, he could not also be courting. And that too was good. It would also be good to be able to use his new weapon in case they were attacked on the move. But White Feathers was talking now, and Wolf turned his attention back.

"Now you have the powder inside, and we push the ball down on it."

They had found that two or three of the thin cloth

patches would provide the necessary tightness, at least on the present temporary basis.

"Now, take the stick and push it down. Be careful not to put your hand over the end, in case the powder fires."

"*Aiee*, it does that sometimes?"

"I have never seen it, but so it is said. I have seen the results."

"Results?"

White Feathers nodded. "One of the traders is called 'Three Fingers.' You will see him. But now, lift the lid of the pan, so . . . a little powder in here. Then shut the lid. Are you ready to shoot?"

"Maybe," Singing Wolf answered nervously.

"Good. Now, point at that white rock on the slope, there. You can look across the little bump at the front. It should look like this."

He sketched a few lines in the dirt with a stick to indicate the sight and the rock that presented a target.

"Now, pull back the flint. You will feel it click. When the picture you see is right, squeeze this little stick with your finger. The gun will push back against your shoulder."

The sparks flashed in the pan, and a fraction of a heartbeat later the gun boomed. Wolf's vision was completely obscured in cottony white smoke.

"Good!" cried White Feathers, who was standing a little aside. "You struck close to the rock!"

"Can we go and look?"

They walked up the slope and found the fresh furrow where the bullet had struck.

"It is good," said White Feathers. "With practice, you will be good. But I have only a little powder. For now, let us clean and load your gun before we break camp. Here, I will give you some of my bullets, and let us find a horn for you to carry powder."

Such generosity was overwhelming.

"Why do you do this for me?" asked Wolf.

"Someone did, for me," explained White Feathers. "You will help someone else. Besides," he went on, "what if we are attacked? I want us well-armed, to save *my* skin."

Both laughed, but Wolf was thinking of the fact that he owed his life to this young man. He wondered if White Feathers also was thinking of this. Was that the reason for the remark about saving his skin?

The first of the big lodges came down by midmorning that next day. It would have been earlier except that it was necessary to wait until the morning's dew was dried by the sun and the heat of the day. It would never do to fold a damp lodge skin. Not only would it be heavier, but it would invite mold and mildew to begin to damage the lodge cover.

By noon, only a couple of skeletons of lodge poles remained, and those were rapidly being disassembled. In a short while, when the signal came to move out, very little was left of the winter camp: a cast-off garment or worn moccasin here and there, ashes of cooking fires, a broken lodge pole.

The column headed westward out into open country. The People would be more comfortable when they could see all of the horizon, the view unobstructed by trees and hills. Double the usual number of wolves circled the procession, scouting ahead and to the sides. An even stronger party of such scouts assisted the young men who drove the loose horses. If the Shaved-heads did attack, surely one of their objectives would be the horse herd.

They traveled slowly, for a number of reasons. They must not appear to be in flight, for that would suggest weakness and would invite attack. In addition, the task of keeping a large number of travelers close together required a slow pace. They must move at the rate of travel of the slowest foot-traveler or the slowest horse-drawn pole-drag. No one must lag behind, because the column stretched thin would suggest to an enemy to attack the middle from the flank, cutting the defense into two groups. This was not discussed openly, but everyone was quite aware. Besides, they were constantly reminded by the presence of the wolves, riding up and down, urging the slower travelers along.

"Come along, close up the space, Uncle." And to the children: "Stay with the column. This is no time to play!"

Much of this was unnecessary, but served to remind each other that it was actually quite a dangerous situation. They were in unfamiliar country, somewhat north of the usual range of the Southern band. Even with White Feathers, to whom this area was familiar, guiding them, it was touchy for a day or two.

There was no doubt that they were followed. The wolves saw mounted riders at a distance from time to time, both behind and on the flanks. The Shaved-heads seemed to make no pretense, actually appearing to show themselves on purpose. It was as if they wished to let the travelers know that they were observed, to keep them nervous and off balance.

To a great extent, it was successful. The People had

expected to be followed, perhaps attacked, and the constant pressure kept stomachs tight and nerves honed to a fine edge. Each day, of course, led the Shaved-heads farther from their own territory. There would come a day, somewhere, when the situation would reverse and the pursuers became the ones in strange territory. Then *they* would be at risk.

But who was to say when and where that would happen? Each day's travel meant more security for the People, and more risk for the Shaved-heads. Hence, less likelihood of attack. It had almost become accepted that the Shaved-heads intended only to see the intruders out of their territory and gone, without further contact. *Almost.*

They had come to a stream that would be a little greater obstacle than they had encountered yet. There was a shallow riffle that would allow pole-drags and even people on foot to cross, but it was narrow. Only one or two abreast could make their way to the other side. To make matters worse, there was not really another place to cross. Deep channels, high cut-banks . . . It was a nervous situation. Twice during the crossing there would be only a few people on one side of the river, virtually defenseless: a short time at the beginning, as the first few reached the west bank, and again at the last. Singing Wolf reflected that *he* would certainly not be comfortable to be the last to cross, knowing that the enemy was just behind him. That dubious honor would fall to those who drove the last of the horses into the water.

He splashed across, dismounted, and stood watching the heavily laden pole-drags clatter across the riffle. He was on a high spot on the west bank, where he could see quite well.

The last of the persons carrying or dragging possessions reached the bank and struggled up the slope. Then the horse handlers began to push the herd toward the water. The crossing was nearly complete. The People were beginning to relax, now in a comparative feeling of safety. There were some laughter and jokes, and someone asked if the band would camp here for the night, though it was early. The problems and risks seemed behind them. They had successfully made the crossing into what seemed their own territory.

Singing Wolf, too, began to relax. He would watch the first of the horses start across and then go and look for his parents.

The first animal, an old gray brood mare, had just entered the water when the attack came.

8

>> >> >>

The first inkling that all was not right was the boom of a musket. It came from the east side of the river. Singing Wolf quickly swept the area with his glance. There was a cloud of white smoke drifting through the timber and bushes to the left, but he did not see the warrior who had fired.

The horses, bunched at the crossing, were milling and plunging nervously, unused to the noise of musket fire. Another gun roared, and as if that were a signal, warriors with shaved heads seemed to rise up out of the bushes. Out of the ground, even. It was a carefully planned ambush. Some of the attackers quickly ran among the horses with ropes, catching a mount, rigging a war bridle with a quick knot and swinging up. Others now charged in, already mounted, and the horse handlers of the People, badly outnumbered, began to scatter in panic. Wolf saw one fall, an arrow jutting from his breast.

The gray mare, leader of the herd, was already halfway across the riffle, and others of the frightened horses broke away to follow her. Some twenty or thirty seemed sure to gain the west bank, while the Shaved-heads tried to cut the herd off so that more would not follow.

One especially skilled enemy horseman rode directly up and down the gravel bar at the riffle, yelling and waving to prevent more horses from crossing. A brave man . . . Singing Wolf suddenly realized that he was lying here on the bank, thinking of himself as an observer. It had not been fear that had immobilized him, though his palms were damp with excitement. It was astonishment, the sheer surprise of the thing. He had never before been under attack and could not seem to function in the confusion. Now a few of the People were responding to the threat. He heard their deep full-throated war cry and felt, rather than saw, men come running from behind him. An arrow arched its way across the river, then another, and two more. The People had the advantage of the higher bank, but the range was too great to be effective. The arrows were falling harmlessly short of their targets.

The terrible realization came that the attackers were gaining control of the milling horses. In a moment, they would be driving off a major part of the herd upon which the Southern band depended. It was their means of hunting buffalo, their source of food, dwellings, clothing . . . the source of their very existence.

Wolf belatedly realized that the one individual horseman in the edge of the stream was the most important factor. That one was preventing more of the People's horses from following the leaders of the herd across the river. As he realized this, Wolf also realized that the warrior was out of the effective range of an arrow. He swung the thunderstick around, praying that he had loaded it properly after the one time he had fired it. He tried to align the sight on the moving figure, and forgot for a moment to draw back the flint. Finally the gun boomed and bucked back against his shoulder. He tried to peer through the smoke, but it took a moment . . . *Aiee!* The horseman still rode up and down. He had missed.

His heart sank, and he began to reload, trying even as he did so to remember the sequence. Powder, patches . . . He was dimly aware that the first of the horses that had crossed the river were pawing their way up the slope to his right. Someone ran up behind him on his left and he turned to glance at the newcomer. It was White Feathers, who threw himself on his belly and pushed his musket in front of him.

"The man at the edge of the river!" yelled Wolf. "I missed him!"

Feathers quickly swept the scene with his glance, nodded, and laid his cheek against the gun's stock. He pulled the flint back, click . . . click . . . and it seemed only a heartbeat's time before the gun roared. Wolf was watching the Shaved-head warrior, who was now knocked from the saddle as if by the slap of a giant hand. *Aiee!* Wolf thought to himself. Aloud, he voiced the war cry as he hurried with his reloading. The still form of the Shaved-head lay spread-eagled below, his lifeblood oozing from a wound in his bare chest to stain the white gravel on which he had ridden his last. The loose horse clattered away, reins dangling.

As it happened, that one musket shot appeared to be the turning point of the fight. The milling horses, now no longer turned back from the river's edge, began to follow their comrades. A couple of the mounted wolves who had been far out on the south flank now came riding in, surprising the Shaved-heads who were trying to drive off the horse herd.

The wolves of the People, riding through timber to join the fight, were apparently taken for a counterattack. Their war cries must have been disconcerting, coming from a new angle. This distraction succeeded, though not on purpose, in allowing the horse herd to begin to break up. Here and there, one or two animals would pull away and plunge into the brush or into the river. The Shaved-heads, who it must be conceded were excellent horsemen, managed to bunch together some thirty or forty animals and start them back eastward. A rider or two of the People started to pursue but quickly realized the danger and pulled back.

"Let them go!" shouted an old woman. "Lives are a poor trade for a few horses!"

The warriors were trying to gather scattered animals in the timber, and people began to splash back across the riffle to look for loved ones. A wail of grief arose, the rising and falling cadence of the Song of Mourning.

"Do not go far alone!" someone warned.

But the Shaved-heads were gone, leaving two dead behind. One had been killed in the surprise charge of the outriders back into the fight. The other, struck down by White Feathers' thunderstick.

The People, too, had suffered losses. Two dead, three with minor wounds. Nearly forty horses. Men were hurrying to check on the presence of favorite animals.

The losses of quality horses were not so severe as might be imagined. Most men, well aware of the value of a favorite buffalo hunter or war-horse, gave special attention to their best animals. Some rode or led such horses while they traveled. All in all, the loose herd was mostly made up of brood mares, young animals not yet broken for use, and pack animals not needed for this move. The loss was not nearly as great as it could have been.

"We will camp here!" The word was passed.

"Set up the lodges?" asked a young woman.

There was discussion, and a trio of women went to find Broken Lance to hear the decision firsthand.

"Yes," nodded the old chief. "It is best. It does not do to hurry until we know where we stand."

"Besides," observed an old woman who shuffled past just then, "it is going to snow."

She pointed to the northwest, where ugly blue-black clouds clumped together like a range of brooding mountains in the distance. The storm front had been overlooked in the excitement of the attack.

"Yes," agreed the old chief. "We will stay here a few days. There is time to make camp before the storm arrives."

As it happened, the People camped there for seven days. The storm's main insult was not snow but ice, a favorite late-season weapon of Cold Maker's. Many trees broke under the weight of the heavy crust of ice that surrounded every limb, every swelling bud, everything that did not move. There was no danger of attack, for travel was impossible. There were many jokes about the poor judgment of the Shaved-heads, who must have been caught in the open by the storm, with only makeshift shelters. At least, the People were snug in their lodges when the fine mist of rain began to freeze to ice on everything it touched.

During the next few days there was much discussion of the attack, and of anything that might have been done differently. In general, the People had been fortunate to have had no greater losses, in horses or in lives. In fact, for several days horses continued to wander in to join the herd, held closely in the timber along the river. Some must have been hiding in the brush, others escaped from the rapidly moving Shaved-heads. There were a couple of mares with small foals, probably rejected by the raiders because they would not travel well. Probably, even, a few abandoned when the ice storm struck, and survival became more important than a few horses.

A couple of things became apparent, though. One was that there were many horses that would never be recovered. Another was that this raid had been much like a warning. The Shaved-heads had not wanted a battle to the death, only to steal a few horses. This was a carefully planned skirmish, a strong suggestion not to winter again in the land of the Shaved-head forest people.

Yet there was one more point that seemed minor at first. It became more important as the tale of the battle was told and retold. It was the matter of the thundersticks.

No one could actually remember for certain that there had been more than a handful of shots fired. Most said only four. But it had been a shot that began the attack, perhaps even as a signal. The outriding wolves had been alerted by the sounds and had ridden back to help with the battle.

A shot, also, may have saved the herd. The attackers were successfully preventing the horses from crossing the river. Mostly, the one young warrior who blocked the riffle, turning the animals back. It was only when he was struck down that the attack began to fall apart. And the shot that put him down was from out of easy bow range. It had come from the thunderstick of the visitor, White Feathers. His skill was recounted again and again around the lodge fires. Once more he was a hero in the eyes of the Southern band.

And once more the realization was like ashes in the mouth of Singing Wolf. He had seen the need first, had tried to do what was required. He had failed. Then had come White Feathers, whose skill had not failed. Once more the visitor had proved himself superior.

How could Wolf expect to compete with such a man? His heart was very heavy.

9

》》 》》 》》

The ice began to melt quickly when the sun rose next morning. There was a short time when the world sparkled with dancing points of light. Each twig and branch, even every dry stalk of grass or herb reflected Sun Boy's torch, and everything was illuminated in splendor.

Singing Wolf was reminded of summer nights when the full moon paints the prairie with its silvery blue, and excitement hangs in the air. It seems a shame to go to bed on such a night. The observer almost expects something special and thrilling to happen, and is afraid that if he is asleep he will miss it. That silvery light is softer, more quiet, though, Wolf reflected. This sparkling world of ice was stirring, dancing, a thing of action. The slightest breeze through the willows produced a tinkling song like a myriad of tiny bells, and the points of sparkling light danced like living things. He wanted to celebrate the excitement of such a morning, but he did not know how. If he were alone, maybe he would have danced. He wondered if there were others who felt as he did, and who would have joined him in the dance to celebrate the beauty of such a morning. He was too self-conscious to pursue it further.

Already, though, the melting had begun. Soon the steady drip of water from every tree sounded like rain along the river. The fat drops from the melting ice joined in little rivulets which eroded more ice as they joined and grew, hurrying toward the stream. By noon, it was apparent that the river was rising. There was now no riffle at all, only an uneven span in the smooth surface of swift water.

It was good to be on the high side of the stream. If any flooding occurred, it would spread to the flat low country on the other bank. And that was good. It would prevent any surprise attack by the Shaved-heads, because they could not cross the flood-swollen stream. It was a time to relax, to smoke and talk and to make plans while the prairie drained and dried enough for travel.

There were many informal discussions about the situation in which they found themselves. It seemed fairly certain that their risk of another raid by the Shaved-heads was quite slim. The forest people had made their point clear, had saved face by stealing a few horses. It was unlikely that the two groups would have another encounter unless the People tried to winter there again. The Eastern band must be warned, of course. Their normal range was closer to that of the Shaved-heads. But White Feathers, who seemed so capable and was so popular in his status as a visitor, would probably tell his people when he rejoined them. Which, of course, Wolf hoped would be soon.

There were many who openly hoped for the romance between White Feathers and young Rain to ripen. It was likely that if it did, White Feathers would move his allegiance to the Southern band, his wife's people, and any group could always benefit from the addition of a bright and handsome young warrior who seemed destined for leadership.

The realization of all of this was quite annoying to Singing Wolf. He was considering a visit for a season with relatives in one of the other bands. The Red Rocks, maybe, whose range was far away to the west.

In a few days the earth was drying, the river receding, and warm breezes were urging forth springs of green everywhere. Soon it would be time to move on, and Broken Lance called for a council.

The formalities were solemnly carried out, and the pipe made its circuit of the council, each in turn offering puffs of smoke and mentally asking success for this deliberation. Broken Lance then opened the discussion.

"My brothers, we had planned to send a trading party to the French, to learn of the thundersticks. We have had to change our plans, as you know, because of contact with the Shaved-heads. Now we must decide what to do next."

"Send a war party! Teach them a lesson!" cried an angry man.

Singing Wolf recognized Short Tail, a few seasons older than he.

Broken Lance stared at the speaker with an exaggerated look of surprise, his eyes wide with wonder. He said nothing for a few moments. *How clever,* thought Singing Wolf; *by his silence, he speaks.* The idea of a war party was not a good one, and most knew it. It was far better to let such a suggestion collapse under its own weight than to argue it.

There was a quiet murmur around the circle, but no one asked to speak.

"Who else speaks for a vengeance raid?" asked the old chief.

Silence.

"I will lead such a raid," said Short Tail, the man who had spoken before. "Who goes with me?"

Again, the silence was heavy. Finally Sand Crossing, a longtime friend of Short Tail, spoke.

"I go," he said simply.

"It is good. Who else?" asked Short Tail.

The silence this time was even more uncomfortable. Fast Turtle, who was seated beside Wolf, leaned over to whisper in his ear.

"Short Tail does not seem as eager as he did."

Wolf nodded, amused. "Will he get any more?"

"I think not. Would *you* follow him?"

The two chuckled quietly. Short Tail, though a good hunter and warrior, was known as a hothead. He would be a valuable follower, but few saw leadership qualities in the young man.

Finally Broken Lance ended the embarrassing silence.

"I am made to think," he observed thoughtfully, "that now is not the best time. Let us speak of it again later, Short Tail."

There were nods around the circle. Broken Lance had once more demonstrated his wisdom and his diplomatic skill. The proposal was dead, but without anger or argument. And even Short Tail had been allowed to escape without undue embarrassment.

"It is good, my chief," he muttered.

"Now," Broken Lance continued, "what of the thundersticks?"

There was an immediate flurry of conversation, and the chief lifted a hand for quiet.

"We have all seen," he said slowly, "that the thunderstick was important in our fight. More than I would have thought, my friends. Only a few shots, but one of them turned the battle. From the edge of the bank, here, our friend White Feathers killed one of their chiefs. A good shot. One that could not have been done with an arrow."

He paused for effect, and allowed the ripple of agreement to make its way around the circle. Then he continued.

"That is not all . . . Those who attacked us had at least two thundersticks, it seems. We heard two, anyway. They had *three* before our Singing Wolf took one. We had no other except that of our visitor. My brothers, we must have more, because others will be trading for them. Without thundersticks we will be helpless. This is not easy for me to admit, for I have grown up in the old ways. But we must change or be left behind. Perhaps even killed."

There were quiet doubts in some of the older faces, and Broken Lance looked for another spokesman to add weight to his opinion.

"Walks in the Sun," he said, "you have traveled far and seen much. Let us hear from you."

The holy man rose. The silvery sheen of the Spanish

bit, the elk-dog medicine of the People, dangled against his chest.

"It is true," he said. "I have seen much, and most of it has made me want to return to our old ways. But look . . . here is the elk-dog medicine bit, worn by the First Horse of our People. I am made to think that there must have been some who opposed the coming of the horse because it was new. Now look! How could we live without our horses? And I must agree with Broken Lance. We may not *like* the noise and smoke and dirty stains of the thunderstick, but we *need* it."

He folded his arms and sat down. There was no one who seemed inclined to challenge such a powerful speech, and Broken Lance spoke again.

"It is good," he said simply. "Now, how do we do this? We have many furs. We had decided to send a party with the furs to trade with the French. But would that now be too dangerous?"

This time there was room for opinion, and a discussion developed quickly. There seemed to be two lines of thought. Some believed that a party of a few men carrying valuable furs would be subject to attack.

"We already know that the Shaved-heads consider us enemies," one man insisted. "They would be proud to kill such a party and steal our furs."

"But we would not be in their country!" insisted another.

"Who knows what they think is theirs?"

"Yes, who knows *what* a Shaved-head might think?"

Broken Lance finally quieted the babble of argument.

"I am made to think," he observed, "that we *must* send such a party. The only question is *when*. Now, furs are not improved by keeping through the summer, no?" He looked around the circle for nods of agreement, and continued. "So we should do so this spring. Yet there may be danger." He paused again and glanced at the faces in the firelight to test the interest and understanding. "So," he went on, "how can we make it safer?"

"Send more men?" someone called.

"Yes, but . . . the more we send, the weaker the main portion of the band."

This did present a problem. At some point the danger to the main body of the Southern band would overshadow the risk to the trading party. But at *what* point?

"Unless," old Broken Lance pondered, "unless we *all* go."

This was a shocking suggestion.

"Into *Eastern* band territory?" a man asked.

"They are our brothers," said another. "It would do no harm."

Broken Lance sat back and watched the spark of an idea grow to a flame. *How clever,* Wolf thought; *everyone believes it was his own idea!* Once more his admiration grew for this wise old leader.

Soon any opposition, any question even, had died down. It was assumed that this would be the course of action. Only the details remained to be decided.

"When?" called someone.

Broken Lance raised a hand for quiet.

"Three days," he said simply.

It had been decided.

10

>> >> >>

So it was decided and carried out. The entire Southern band, staying together for safety, would travel northward with the migrating geese. They would be out of their own territory, but in an area well known to the Eastern band. White Feathers would act as their guide.

This was one more thorn in the flesh of Singing Wolf. It was becoming intolerable, the presence of this man with the Southern band. Surely, there had never been a young warrior who rose so rapidly in prestige. And it seemed so undeserved. What did the man have to offer that he, Wolf, did not? Well, the knowledge of the thunderstick, he must admit. But that could be learned. Yet here was the visitor, living in the lodge of the chief, his advice sought by the leaders of the Southern band. White Feathers was actually being asked to *lead* the Southern band this spring. Well, it was his territory through which they now traveled. This was no different than a war party or hunting party, led by a minor warrior because of his specific skills for that venture.

At least, thought Wolf, this responsibility kept White Feathers busy and occupied. The man could do little courting when he was busy with things of leadership. At times when Wolf's thinking was at its clearest he could tell himself that jealousy was at the root of his dislike. White Feathers had come between Wolf and his lifelong friend, Rain. He did not really believe it, of course. His mind might accept such a thing, but not his heart. Yet, try as he would, he could really find nothing bad or evil about the man. White Feathers had saved his life, and there had been no way to repay the debt.

But every contact since then had seemed to lessen the prestige of Singing Wolf and to enhance that of the visitor. It was frustrating beyond belief to try to find something to criticize in the man, and to find only good.

Rain . . . Wolf had seen her very little all winter, and now, as the band moved on, he found himself avoiding her entirely. That was not a very smart thing to do, he finally realized. He could have been avidly courting her while White Feathers busied himself with the older men and the politics of the band. It might have been a great opportunity, and once more he had failed to see it. The ugly suspicion occurred to him that maybe he *was* deficient. Maybe White Feathers was actually far more intelligent, as well as handsome. Wolf felt shy and embarrassed.

He thought of going now to talk to Rain, hoping to repair the shattered friendship. He decided that he could not risk it. While there was still a doubt, all was not lost. But if he approached the girl, she might easily rebuke him. Her last words to him had been angry, and he saw nothing to change that. She might even laugh at him, at his presumption that he had enough prestige to even talk to her. Maybe, even, she and White Feathers had come to an understanding, and would marry after the trading mission. He had heard no rumors, but who would tell *him*? Fast Turtle, maybe. No, Turtle was his friend and would not want to hurt him.

Maybe he could ask Fast Turtle if there were rumors of such a romance. Wolf quickly abandoned that idea. He was afraid of what he might learn. So he continued to suffer, trying to conceal his pain.

The band traveled well, and good weather held as they moved northward and now a little to the east. They were out of the area inhabited by the Shaved-heads now. Any people they might meet would probably be Kenzas, who were known to the Eastern band through long association and were considered friendly.

"They are growers," White Feathers explained, "though they do have a fall hunt sometimes."

"Where do they hunt?" a man asked.

"West, into the prairie. Along the River of Swans, sometimes. They know our Northern band along the river that has their name . . . River of Kenzas."

"Do they trade with the French?" asked Wolf.

"Yes, some, I think. But they do not hunt furs as much as we do. The French want furs and robes, not corn and pumpkins. Well, some of that . . ."

It was a constant topic for discussion, what they would find at the French outpost. The People had accumulated a large number of furs during the past season and were eager to learn their value in trade. Beaver, otter, mink, a few tanned robes of buffalo. White Feathers had attempted to show those who were interested in trapping how to prepare the skins for trade.

"A beaver should be round, stretched on a hoop."

"*Aiee!* Beavers are not round!"

"True, but this is as the traders want them."

"Otter, too?"

"No, otter should be skinned from the rear, not cut up the belly. Dry it on a stick shaped like this . . ."

He had demonstrated how to bend a stick of dogwood in a long and slender loop with an open end. This would be similar to the treatment of mink, using a smaller stick. There were those among the People who dimly remembered these things. It had only been a generation since the trade with the Spanish at Santa Fe.

"What about the raccoon?" someone asked. "Round, like beaver, or long and in a tube like otter?"

"Neither," White Feathers answered. "The raccoon is not as valuable as the others, but when they do want it, raccoon is square."

There was a shout of laughter.

"*Square?*"

"Yes . . . it is true. They want it to be square. The Sky-eyes have strange ways, do they not? But as it is said, when you visit someone's lodge, you eat his food, follow his ways. If it is not forbidden by yours, of course."

Singing Wolf was sickened by the way that people hung on the visitor's every word, laughing at his little jokes and urging him on. It was getting worse as they neared the area where the traders were presumed to be living. Along with the blind adulation of White Feathers' knowledge, skill, and wit, his prestige seemed to continue growing. Many an argument among the People was now terminated with a remark such as "Well, White Feathers has said so!" For such a claim there was virtually no answer. What could one say?

One evening as shadows grew long and the campfires blossomed like orange flowers in the gathering dusk, Wolf could stand it no longer. He must get away to think. He climbed alone to a little bald-topped hill behind the camp. He leaned against a sun-warmed rock, watching the shifting colors of the sunset. There was still too much of winter's chill in the earth to make sitting comfortable. So he stood, leaning, enjoying the beauty of the evening.

Trees in the valley below were showing the varying colors of new green as they woke from winter's sleep. High overhead a long line of geese headed northward. He wondered where they would camp for the night.

There was a sound below him as someone approached. He had wanted to be alone, and now he had a sudden urge to hide, to sneak away, to avoid any contact. *No,* he told himself, *I was here first. Let him find another place.*

The intruder was approaching from the direction of the camp, so Wolf did not even consider any danger from outside. He had carried his bow and arrows, but held them casually, watching the dim path where the newcomer would appear. Ah, there . . . a woman . . . *Aiee,* Rain!

A confusion of thoughts ran quickly through his mind. She had come to see him, to apologize for her foolishness. No, she merely wanted to talk to him. Maybe she did not know he was here, and she, too, wished to get away to think. He glanced around wondering if it would be possible to slip away . . . No, too late.

Then she saw him, and it was plain that she was surprised. Her reason for being here, then, was definitely not to see him, talk to him, or apologize. Maybe . . . *Aiee!* Maybe she was here to meet White Feathers! The hurtful thought gnawed at his belly and he wished he could sink into the ground.

She stopped a few feet away.

"*Ah-koh,* Wolf."

He nodded, embarrassed.

"I did not know you were here," she said quietly. Her voice was like the whisper of the breeze in the tallgrass prairie in autumn. "I did not mean to bother you."

"It is nothing," he said. "I was leaving."

"I have seen you very little."

"Yes. I have been busy."

"I heard of your thunderstick," she said conversationally. "You did not bring it tonight?"

He glanced at his bow. "No, I have very little powder and lead."

He did not add that what he did have was a gift from White Feathers. She would know that, he supposed. He wondered if they talked of him sometimes when they were together. Probably, and probably as a joke. *Aiee,* he wished he were somewhere else. Anywhere.

She seemed friendly enough, but very cool, distant. His greatest fear was that he would say or do something utterly stupid. Close on the heels of that fear was another. At any moment White Feathers might arrive for their tryst. He could hardly calm himself in his anxiety over that.

"You have wintered well," she observed.

"Yes, the trapping was good." He knew that was not what she meant. He had seen her eyes glance over his buckskin-clad form.

Wolf was in good shape, he knew. He had worked hard at his traps, and his muscles had hardened as the excess fat melted away. But for her to notice his appearance now, when it was over for them, was only another hurt.

He looked at Rain in the soft light. She had never been more beautiful, he thought. Her trim body filled her buckskin dress, each curve pushing gently against appropriately yielding softness. He swallowed hard.

"You, too, have wintered well." He knew that she was well aware of his meaning.

It was pure torture to stand here and talk this way. She was so beautiful, yet so distant, so different from the lifelong friend he had known.

"Have you . . ." He started to ask if she and White Feathers had made plans, but could not bring himself to do so. He would be unable to bear listening to the details if her answer was affirmative.

"What?" she asked, bewildered.

"Have you . . . have you eaten yet?" he mumbled.

There, he had done it. Said something unbelievably stupid.

"Yes," Rain answered, puzzled. "Why?"

Maybe, he thought, this was a way to escape before her suitor arrived.

"Well, I have not," he announced. "My parents will worry about me. Maybe I should go home."

"Maybe so . . ." she answered tentatively, still puzzled.

Wolf was totally embarrassed now. He had made one utterly stupid remark and then, to conceal it, had blundered into an even worse one. *Aiee,* she would never again look at him without feeling disgust and amusement. If Rain had still had any feeling at all for him, he must have just destroyed it. Numbly, he turned and started down the hill.

Maybe, he thought, he could go and visit relatives in the Northern band. Better yet, the Mountain band, who were farther away. Let someone else do the fur trading for him. At least he would not run the risk of such a hurtful encounter as he had just survived. And he would be spared the triumphs of his rival, who seemed destined only to grow in prestige.

11

>> >> >>

It was only a few days until the travelers reached the area they sought. They had encountered several members of the Eastern band, hunters who were, by ones and twos, working off pent-up energy from a long winter. Some made no pretense of serious hunting. They were merely out, moving around with the restlessness that afflicts humans at the time of the migration of the geese.

What is it, this thrill of excitement, which strikes twice yearly? No one can watch the long lines across the sky, heading south in autumn and back north in the spring, without a sense of wonder. Where are they going? Where have they been? What far places have they seen? Is there a sort of racial memory, an instinct that whispers in the human soul: *Go, go with them and see?* The very cries of the great birds echo the call, sending a shiver up the spine, an unreasonable urge to drop all responsibility and *go*. How many humans, through the eons of time, have listened to this primitive trumpet call and followed? Some have in this way seen wondrous things, new lands, made great discoveries. Others, not so fortunate or with lesser guidance, perished on some windswept tundra, still seeking an answer to the primordial urge to follow the geese.

This was one of the urges that thrust itself upon young Singing Wolf that spring. Life was becoming more and more complicated. The encounter with Rain on the hilltop had affected him deeply. Wolf did not want another such accidental meeting. He dreaded, too, the almost daily encounters with White Feathers, cheerful, confident, helpful. He did not want this. It was bad enough to owe the young man his life while he still resented Rain's budding romance. It was even worse to be unable to find anything at all for which he could criticize or even dislike his rival. That in truth was the frustration he faced. How good it would be, he thought, to be able to leave all these concerns behind, to start anew, a new beginning. If he could leave it all, his family, friends, his worries, to follow the flight of the geese.

He would even leave his thunderstick. It had come to symbolize the unpleasantness that had to do with White Feathers. Yes, he would give it to his friend Fast Turtle . . . let it become Turtle's problem, while he, Wolf, followed the geese. Then his thoughts returned to the real world, and to the realization that such things were only a fantasy. He could not do it.

So they traveled on. They did not encounter the main body of the Eastern band. White Feathers sent word to his family by some of the hunters that he was well, and of the nature of their mission. He would stay with the Southern band until the Sun Dance, when all bands would gather for the annual festival.

Word quickly swept through the band that this was White Feathers' intention. It was not good news to Singing Wolf. *Aiee,* it was just the Moon of Greening! Two moons, nearly three, until the traditional gathering in the Moon of Roses. And these, in one of the most romantic times of the year! Wolf was certain that the purpose of White Feathers in remaining with this band was that of courtship. It was not good.

Then there came a day when White Feathers announced that the French settlement they sought was only two sleeps away. There was great excitement. Wolf was pleased, because in a way this signified the end of part of his dependence on White Feathers. He would acquire his own powder and lead, instruction about his thunderstick. He could practice with it, become as skilled as White Feathers. Better, maybe.

He got out the thunderstick and wiped it with a greasy rag, looking it over carefully. He was not sure what to look for, but in the action of caring for the weapon he was attempting to show respect. Surely its spirit would understand. He had wrapped the gun in a piece of buckskin to keep it from the moisture of morning dews. White Feathers had suggested it. Now he began to wonder. Would it not be a good idea to have a case for the weapon? Like a pipe case or a bow case . . . Yes, for the same purpose! It could be ornamented and fringed. Once more his interest in the thunderstick was rekindled. He sought out Running Deer that evening as they camped.

"Mother, I would ask you of an idea I have."

"Yes?"

"This thunderstick . . ."

"Yes . . . I am not sure that I approve."

"I understand that, Mother. But it is here. We must accept it or suffer from the hands of those who do."

Running Deer nodded. "I know, my son. But mothers must say such things. Probably the mother of the man who made the first bow felt so."

Her eyes twinkled, and Wolf realized that she was teasing him. She had used this way to remind him to be careful with the new weapon. Now she spoke again.

"What did you want to tell me about the thunderstick?" she asked.

"Oh . . . nothing about it, really. Only, I am made to think, Mother, of a case to protect it."

"Ah! Like a bow case!"

"Yes, much like that."

"Here, hold it up. *Aiee,* I am not sure I should touch it. Are there taboos?"

"Only the usual, I think, about women touching weapons."

She nodded.

"No matter, then. I am past the time of menstruating. Let me see . . ."

Gingerly at first, then with more interest, she studied the weapon as her son held it, speaking half to herself.

"Yes . . . like a bow case . . . narrower at one end . . . a flap at the wider open end . . . ties . . ."

She paused, touching the polished wood and the shiny mechanism gently. She smiled at him.

"You know, Wolf, it does have a strange beauty about it.

And to honor it with a case . . . yes, it is good. Let me see what I have. And here, I will measure."

As she spoke, she was taking measurements with a thong. Length . . . width, at both wide and narrow ends. She hummed softly as she knotted her thong to save the dimensions.

"There! It is good! I have the measures I need, and I will begin tonight. You know, though, I cannot do much until we camp."

"Yes, I know. Thank you, Mother."

"Well, White Feathers says we will be there in two sleeps. Then I will have more time."

"Yes, so it is said."

Even here, he thought, *in my own parents' lodge, I must hear of White Feathers!*

But it was good to be thinking of other things, and of how the case would look on the thunderstick. He re-wrapped it and put it away.

The stockade of the trading post was built of logs set on end in the ground. It was square, perhaps thirty steps on each side. Outside the enclosure, a few lodges and various kinds of makeshift shelters were scattered across the meadow. People were coming and going, people in differ-ent sorts of garments and hats and carrying various weap-ons. Singing Wolf was astonished at the bustle and confu-sion.

Upstream, a few bow shots away, was one of the towns of the Kenzas, their log and mud lodges dug partly into the ground. Downstream, a long open flat, partially en-closed by a bend of the river, provided enough room for hundreds of lodges, with grass for the horses beyond.

White Feathers pointed. "We can camp there," he indicated.

In a short while the first of the big lodges were raising their pointed tops toward the sky. By dusk the glow of lodge fires was showing red through the skin covers of each newly erected lodge. This was now home, made so by the ritual of the first fires in a new camp. It was a message to the spirits of the place, an announcement: *Here am I, here I will be,* accompanied by the small gift of a pinch of tobacco to honor the spirits, a plea for permission and approval. By dark, everyone was settling in quite comfortably.

There would be no trading until tomorrow, but some of the young men walked over to the stockade to see what was going on. There were several fires, with groups of people gathered around exchanging stories and recounting the events of the winter just past.

Singing Wolf was fascinated by the mixture of language and dress that was in evidence. There were several different tribes or nations represented here, judging from the variety of patterns of shirts and leggings. And moccasins! It had never occurred to him how many different ways there must be to make a moccasin. Those of the People were hard-soled with untanned rawhide. The softer uppers were stitched with sinew, and any decoration was sewn to the soft part with quills pounded flat and dyed in different colors. The traditional height of the People's footwear was the turned-down cuff a finger-breadth above the ankle bones. Here he saw moccasins that reached to just below the knee, some that ended below the ankle bone, and everything between. There were some, even, in which the sole leather was soft, drawn upward around the instep, and stitched to a small disc of leather in front. These, said White Feathers, were forest people from farther east. "Puckered-moccasin People," he called them.

The garments of the French traders were of even greater variety than those of the different tribes. Their hats, too, were worthy of note. Some were fur caps. Others seemed to be woven of some material like that of a blanket, but which stretched to fit tightly around the head. Still others were broad flat headgear with a wide brim that extended all the way around the head.

Their shirts, too . . . Some were of a fine white cloth with a loose-fitting open jacket of darker material. Other traders wore rougher clothing, some even buckskins like those of the natives. Most surprising to Wolf was a sort of legging or pantaloon that reached only to the knee, where it was drawn tightly with a string. Below that, a skintight covering of white which covered the calves and ankles, and shoes of leather.

Of course, he was fascinated by the eyes of these outsiders, the Sky-eyes. Even by firelight, the light color of the eyes of many of them could be seen. There had once been an adopted member of the People, he had heard, who was called Sky-Eyes. He wondered if that man, a respected warrior of the Southern band a few generations ago, had been one of these French.

He also wondered whether the French had learned to speak the tongues of all the nations that he saw represented here. That question virtually answered itself as he passed one of the fires. One of the French traders, in a fur cap, white shirt, and buckskin leggings, was talking to a mixed group, gesturing actively with hand signs.

Of course! thought Wolf. *How simple. Nearly everyone knows hand signs.*

Another question had no answer quite so simple. Here were gathered people from a large number of tribes and nations. Some would probably be enemies. Was there not likely to be fighting? He wondered but did not want to ask. Finally, one of the other young men in the group voiced the question.

"No, that is no problem," answered White Feathers. "This is a neutral place. Even enemies will not fight here. Otherwise there could be no trading."

It must be, Wolf decided, as it sometimes happened when the band was traveling. They would be strung out across the prairie, with pole-drags and women and children. Sometimes they encountered a similar band of some other tribe. Maybe not an enemy, but an unknown, possibly dangerous. Neither group would wish to risk harm to the women and children, so both would stop. Two or three leaders from each group would meet halfway and talk in hand signs. Not of war, but of weather, the season, the hunt. Small talk. By mutual consent, there would be avoidance of the risk to their families. Not a spoken agreement, just an understanding.

This, Singing Wolf now decided, must be much the same. A place in which a temporary truce would avoid much risk, yet allow the trade that everyone needed.

12
»» »» »»

The experience of the trading post was almost over-whelming. Sights, sounds, and smells that were completely foreign . . . Boxes and bales and barrels of goods such as they had never seen . . . There were piles of furs, their pungent yet familiar scents mingling with those of tobacco and leather and the new wool of blankets and clothing.

It was not too busy. The trade had not yet been well enough established to attract the large numbers of trappers and traders who would assemble each spring in later years. This was a tentative, probing operation on the part of the French, to explore the financial possibilities in such a venture. It was in the best interest of the traders to treat fairly anyone who came to trade. There would come a time when the lure of financial gain would destroy this trust, but to these early traders an openhanded honesty was all-important. Anyone who felt that he had been treated unfairly would not return, and would tell his story to everyone he met.

So far, relations had been good. There had been a few muskets in the hands of the Pawnees and the Kenzas for several years. Now, more were being introduced, along with other trade items. Blankets, knives and steel fire-strikers, of course, but also other objects of esthetic value and daily usefulness. Glass beads, to replace porcupine quills in the delicate embroidery work so prized on wearing apparel by the people of the plains. Needles of steel to replace bone sewing awls. Small mirrors, polished ornaments. Tobacco, a staple item carried by every traveling trader, used for recreational smoke as well as ritual offerings to the spirits.

This was only a beginning. Soon other goods would appear for trade . . . sugar, tea, salt, as well as more complicated objects of adornment such as tiny hawks' bells and silver dangles. But that was yet to come.

Singing Wolf stood in the big room, staring in awe at the vast array of goods stacked, piled, and hanging everywhere. At the suggestion of White Feathers, he had brought only a few skins on this first visit, to show the quality of his season's catch.

"*Ah-koh!*" someone said.

He turned to see a smiling trader in a white shirt, leather vest, and pantaloons, with white hose above his moccasins. *A strange mixture of garments*, thought Wolf. By the day's end, however, *no* mixture of apparel would seem unusual. The trader was speaking now, in a tongue unknown to Singing Wolf.

"No!" signed Wolf. "I do not know your tongue."

The other nodded pleasantly.

"It is no matter," he signed. "What is your nation? How are you called?"

The man was quite skilled in the use of hand signs, it seemed.

"I am Singing Wolf. Elk-dog People . . . Southern band."

"Ah, yes, I heard your Southern band was here. You have wintered well?"

Singing Wolf nodded. This was no time to go into the details of their conflict with the Shaved-heads.

"I am called Three Fingers," the trader went on, displaying the reason by showing his maimed right hand. The index finger was missing, only a stump remaining at the knuckle. He wiggled it comically, then placed the stump at his nose and twisted it solemnly. This maneuver looked as if the missing finger was inside the nose. Onlookers roared with laughter. It was apparently a common stunt, played for the astonishment of newcomers.

Singing Wolf was at a loss for a moment, but recovered to comment with hand signs.

"You are well-named."

"Yes. It is not really good. See?"

The trader briefly illustrated how the use of his thumb and middle finger left something to be desired. It would be clumsy.

"I show you this to remind you," he went on, "be careful when you load your gun."

Wolf nodded. It was a lesson not to be forgotten.

"Now, let us look . . . You have skins to trade?"

"Yes." He handed a prime otter pelt to the trader, who stroked it, turned it over, smelled it, and finally nodded.

"It is good. Not the best, maybe."

Fast Turtle, who stood near, was indignant. *"Aiee!* In his life, he has never seen better!" he growled.

It was true. The hard winter had produced thick fur, soft and sleek, and this was one of the best.

"I know, Turtle. We are trading!" said Wolf, aside.

The People were no strangers to this occupation. Traveling traders had crisscrossed the plains for many generations before the first Europeans. Any commodity available to any tribe or nation was theoretically available to all. Does not the red pipestone, used by all for medicine pipes, come from only one quarry in the north? And a tribe to the northwest of the Elk-dog nation was, in hand signs, the "Nation of Traders" in recognition of their skill and their love for trading.

Wolf was watching the trader carefully as this exchange took place. He was certain that the trader understood the game, after his last remark. The buyer downgrades the quality of the offered goods; the seller upgrades it. Even Fast Turtle's remark was part of the game.

In this case, however, it provided another benefit. For an instant, a mere fraction of a heartbeat, there had been a flash of amusement in the eyes of the Frenchman. It showed that he was, indeed, skilled at the game. In addition, Wolf had the strong feeling that Three Fingers had *understood* the exchange between the two young men of the People. Yet, he had so far used only hand signs.

"You know our tongue," Wolf accused, without hand signs. It was a statement, not a question.

The trader smiled. "Yes, a little. But it helps to learn what one can."

Yes, thought Wolf, *this, too, is part of the game.* He nodded. "Now," he said seriously, "let us trade."

"It is good. You have more furs?"

"A few."

Keep the trader guessing.

"And you want . . . what?"

Singing Wolf placed the thunderstick on the trader's table.

"Powder, lead, for this."

Three Fingers picked up the gun, turned it over, and examined it.

"Where did you get this?" he asked. "Your band has not traded here before."

"That is true. I took it from a man who tried to kill me. He was . . ."

The trader held up a hand in protest.

"No, I do not want to know. I must be a friend to all. You have it . . . it is yours! Now, you have a bullet mold?"

"No. A few bullets. They seem too small."

He rolled a couple of the silvery balls out on the table. The trader took one, compared it to the weapon's bore.

"Yes, too small. Where did you get these?"

"A . . . a friend."

"Yes . . ."

Three Fingers had turned and was rummaging on a shelf. He turned back to the table with a big metal spoon, a tonglike tool, and a chunk of shiny metal, half as big as a fist.

"You know how to use these?"

"I . . ." Wolf paused for a moment. White Feathers would teach him. It would be easy just to say, "Of course," and then ask Feathers. But his pride was at stake. He could face a little loss of pride with this stranger better than . . . "No!" he said quickly. "I have had the thunderstick only a short while. Can you show me?"

The trader looked at him for a moment, as if surprised. Then he looked around the room, and called to one of the other traders who was busy handling loose furs, sorting and stacking them. They exchanged a few words, and the other man nodded and waved. Three Fingers turned back to his customer.

"Come, we will go outside. Bring your gun. We will put your furs here." He placed the sample furs on a shelf. "We finish trading later." Then he led the way outside, followed by Wolf and Fast Turtle.

A couple of bow shots away from the post, Three Fingers stopped, laid down the things he was carrying, and began to gather sticks for a fire. Wolf understood, and joined in the effort. In a short while the flames from the trader's tinder had begun to flicker up through the smaller sticks, and then larger chunks. He waited for the fire to subside somewhat, then took the big spoon or dipper. He placed the lead ingot in it and carefully nestled it into the glowing coals.

"Now, we let it melt," he stated, settling himself and lighting his pipe with a stick from the fire. "Is your thunderstick loaded?"

"Yes."

"You have fired it, no?"

"Twice."

Three Fingers nodded.

"I missed," Wolf admitted.

"Yes, but your bullets did not fit. That will help." He paused a moment. "Fire your gun to empty it," he suggested. "Aim at the tree there, with the knot on this side."

He pointed to a tree some twenty paces away. A gnarled burl was plainly visible, egg-sized and pointing directly toward them, at about shoulder height. Wolf raised the weapon, checked the powder in the pan, and lowered the frizzen again. He aimed and squeezed the trigger lever, and the gun boomed.

Three Fingers jumped to his feet. "Let us see!" he called over his shoulder, striding toward the tree.

The bullet had struck a hand's span from the knot, high and to the right.

"It is good!" insisted the trader. "The proper bullets . . . you will see!"

Until midday, the two melted lead and cast bullets, loaded and fired. By early afternoon, Wolf was becoming proficient in cutting the sprue from newly cast balls, loading the weapon, and in firing accurate shots at his target. After three bullets had grouped in an area that could be covered by the palm of a hand, Fast Turtle was impressed.

"*Aiee!*" he said softly.

Three Fingers shrugged.

"It is good! You are ready."

They returned to the trading post, and Wolf went to bring his other furs. For some time, then, they settled down to serious trading. More powder and lead, a bright blanket, a knife. With a little credit he had left, Wolf obtained a mirror and some needles for his mother, as well as some glass beads. They would look nice on his gun case. A twist of tobacco for his father . . .

Fast Turtle, who had only a few furs, traded for a knife and tobacco, and promised to bring enough next season so that he, too, could have a thunderstick.

The trader watched the two walk away toward the lodges of the People.

"Pierre," one of the other traders said to Three Fingers, "you spent much time with that one."

"Yes, but I think that one is special. He is wise, his gun was well-cared-for and greased, even before he knew much about it. He learns fast. Mostly, though, he knew when to ask my help. It takes a real man to know that."

13
» » »

The People spent several days at the trading station of the French. There was much to see and do, much to learn. Besides the French fur traders with their strange dress and customs, there were people of several different tribes not usually encountered by the Southern band. It was a source of great amusement to gather with these strangers to exchange traditional stories and legends. Usually a storyteller would use his own language, augmented with hand signs.

Creation stories were among the favorites, usually the first exchanged. The familiarity of retelling was exciting to the young. They had heard countless times how the People came into the world through a hollow cottonwood log, summoned by a deity. The children always squealed with delight when someone who had never heard their story asked about whether they were still coming through. It was a challenge to the storyteller to induce some listener to ask. Then it was possible to use the private joke, a delight to the People when it worked well.

"Are your people still coming through?" some stranger would ask, in a gentle fun-making way.

"Of course not," the storyteller could then respond. "A fat woman got stuck in the log and no more could come through. That is why ours has always been a small nation."

Then the crowd around the story fire would roar with laughter at the success of the storyteller's use of the old joke. Some storytellers were more adept at drawing the listeners into the story, inducing them to ask. It would become a game, the People watching and listening to see whether the uninitiated listener would be persuaded to raise the question.

Singing Wolf and Fast Turtle sat in the rear ranks of the circle, half-listening and whispering quietly.

"It is a good night," observed Turtle. "Some of these stories I have never heard before."

Wolf nodded. "Yes. The one about climbing into the world on the roots of a giant grapevine sounds much like ours, no?"

"That is true. I wonder if the French will tell theirs."

"Who knows? But some of them are here. Ah! Here comes the part about Fat Woman!"

They waited anxiously as the storyteller told of the Old Man, astride the log, tapping with a drumstick. With each tap on the log, another of the People crawled out to stand upright in the sunlight. Skillfully, the story seemingly unfinished, the storyteller paused, waiting, looking around the circle. There was only silence.

"Will anyone ask?" Turtle whispered.

Wolf shrugged. "Maybe."

"If no one does, will he tell of Fat Woman?"

"I do not know. But Spotted Dog is good. Someone will ask."

"It is said," Turtle whispered, "that our ancestor Pale Star was the most skilled ever at drawing in the listener."

"Be still, Turtle! We will miss it!"

Just then an old man on the far side of the circle cleared his throat to speak.

"Are they still coming through?" he called.

"No, it was not to be. A fat woman became lodged in the log, and no one has come through since. *Aiee,* we are a small nation."

The laughter rippled around the circle. It had been skillfully done. Just the right amount of self-deprecation, just a touch of sadness.

Wolf noticed something else. The old man who had asked the question was one of the storytellers. Earlier, he had told the story of his own people's creation. Wolf had the odd feeling that the old man already knew about Fat Woman. Had he asked only to help Spotted Dog with *his* story? An interesting thought . . . Maybe Dog had asked the other in advance, to assist him. No, surely not. But they *were* fellow storytellers, though their people had different customs. The old storyteller had called out in the tongue of the People, however. If he had had enough contact to speak their tongue, would he not have heard the Fat Woman joke? Of course!

This was a great revelation to Wolf. Maybe, he thought,

that was part of the joke. One who knew the story was *expected* to ask.

He was still thinking about it when Turtle elbowed his ribs.

"There is Rain!" he pointed.

"Do not point, Turtle."

"Why not?"

"Never mind."

He had not noticed the presence of the girl before. It must be that she had just arrived. She sat with her mother, almost directly across the fire, near the front ranks. Unconsciously, Wolf drew back in the shadows a little, and then wondered why he had done so.

Wolf was pleased that Rain sat with her mother and not with White Feathers. He was trying to adjust to the obvious fact that Feathers was pressing the courtship. The lilting melodies of the courting flute were frequently heard outside the camp. Wolf felt quite helpless in the face of such competition. If he only had *time.* Now that he too was armed with the latest in weaponry, was he not as much a man as White Feathers?

Maybe he should learn to play the flute . . . No, that would be too obvious. Wolf had been torn almost constantly by the torment of knowing that White Feathers' courtship was going on. There was a constant gnawing in his belly whenever he thought of it. Rain, his lifelong friend, in the embrace of another . . . *aiee,* it was painful! He had tried not to think about it. It helped some to throw himself into other activities, like becoming familiar with his thunderstick. But not much.

He still found himself avoiding contact with Rain, because the hurt was so great when he saw her. Shining, beautiful, yet so unattainable for him. And her beauty tonight was beyond belief. It may have been the medicine of the flickering fire . . . no, not that. This was real. Rain really *was* the most beautiful woman in the world. How could it be denied?

And once more, close on the heels of that realization, came the hopeless thought that she was unavailable, completely out of reach for him.

One thing was certain. He could not gain her attention by avoiding her, as he had been doing. Maybe it was that night, the night when his attitude began to change. He was still glum and not optimistic about it, but he came to one realization there by the fire that evening. He would do *something*. He was not certain yet just what it would be, but something that would at least give him a chance to recover the woman who had been his friend and potential lover.

What harm could there be in trying? He had already been made to look ineffective, at least in his own eyes. He had already lost her. To try to recover her affection would hurt greatly if he failed. But how could it be worse than the pain that now gnawed at his gut? He had nothing to lose.

Wolf was never certain exactly how it happened that night when his thinking changed. Possibly it was in sheer desperation. He became determined. He was far from confident, but at least he resolved to try. Tomorrow he would seek out Rain and talk to her. He would demand a statement as to her feelings. *No!* He must not do that. He feared what her answer would be, and if her words went against him, it would be over. No, if he could maintain contact, but prevent her from declaring herself . . . Yes, that would be the way. Until she announced her intention, there was hope that this terrible time of doubt would still have a favorable outcome.

He wished that he could talk with someone. His father? No, he could not imagine Walks in the Sun in such a situation. Certainly not Fast Turtle, who had even less experience, less confidence, than Wolf himself. If there were someone, an older man who could give him advice . . . Someone like Strong Bow, maybe, who was considered skilled in the ways of women.

Strong Bow, now middle-aged, had but one wife, it was true, but she was Pawnee. It was said that Pawnee women had complete choice with whom they slept, and by the standards of the People, their behavior was sometimes scandalous. Yet this Pawnee woman, Pretty Sky, who was still one of the most attractive in the camp, had chosen Strong Bow. Not only that, she had chosen to leave her own people to follow him. Was that not a great tribute to his skill as a lover? And she was completely faithful!

Even as he pondered this, Wolf knew that he could not ask such advice. To do so would be an invasion of privacy. No, that would be like asking, "Uncle, how is it in bed?" Such a thing would be completely inappropriate. In matters of the heart, he decided, it must be that one walks alone.

He found himself staring at the beautiful face across the fire. Rain's eyes sparkled in the firelight, interested, totally absorbed in the story that unfolded. She seemed unaware of Wolf's eyes upon her. *Aiee,* such beauty, such perfection . . .

A log burned in two, fell into the fire, and sent a shower of dancing sparks against the dark sky, to join the countless points of light already scattered there. Somewhere, a night bird called, and from the thicker timber downstream he heard the hollow cry of *Kookooskoos,* the hunting owl who calls his own name.

The world is good, Wolf thought. Now, if he could only find the way to share it again with Rain, as they had done when they were children in the Rabbit Society.

14

>> >> >>

"**W**here will you go now?" asked Three Fingers.

The Southern band was preparing to move on.

"To the Sun Dance," Wolf answered. "Then, summer camp."

"And where will you winter?"

"*Aiee*, I do not know, Three Fingers! That is far down the trail."

Singing Wolf had become quite comfortable with the trader. He had been treated fairly and had received good advice and instruction. He had practiced enough with the thunderstick that he was becoming an excellent marksman. This seemed to impress the Frenchman, and gained him extra attention.

"Why do you ask of our winter camp?" Wolf inquired. "Would you come to visit us?"

The trader smiled and considered for a moment.

"Maybe, but probably not. I need to stay here. No, I only wondered if you would be looking for furs."

"Of course. There will be furs wherever we are. Otter, fox . . ."

"Beaver?"

"Yes, beaver. That is your greatest want?"

"I think so. Beaver has more value. You use a deadfall?"

"Yes. Some use different kinds."

The trader nodded.

"And you say others of your people will bring more?"

"Maybe so. They are interested, they like the goods that you have to trade. Not only guns and powder, but beads . . ."

Wolf held up his gun, in its new case, just finished by his mother. It was a work of art, fine white buckskin decorated not only with the traditional quills but with the newer glass beads.

"That is very special . . . strong medicine," observed Three Fingers. "Yes, I can see that we need more of these things."

"There may be too many people trapping for skins," observed Wolf.

"How could that be?"

"Not enough beaver and otter."

"There will be more," the trader insisted.

"Of course. But you do not understand, Uncle."

The trader looked a little surprised at Wolf's use of this term of respect. It was directed to any adult male older than one's self. But there was probably only a few winters' difference in their ages. A more common usage would be to address a wise old elder as "Uncle." Flattered, the trader let it pass, and Wolf perhaps did not even realize the significance of his usage.

"There are too many people," he went on. "Look . . . maybe forty lodges. It is a problem just to feed their horses through the winter."

The trader looked puzzled.

"But I do not see . . ."

"*Aiee,* if everyone traps beaver, there will be traps everywhere, more traps than beaver, no? It would be dangerous, maybe. I might stumble into someone else's deadfall!"

"Ah . . . I see. Some need to go farther from the camp, no?"

"Maybe," agreed Wolf, "but how far? A day out and back . . . The snows . . . Cold Maker is treacherous. There might also be enemies."

Now the trader seemed to understand. He nodded.

"I can see . . . yes, it will be a change. But I need the *plews* . . . skins. Anyway, you will come back?"

"Of course. I will need more powder, maybe."

Both chuckled.

"Keep it dry!" advised Three Fingers.

Wolf nodded. "I will try!"

He turned to go, and the trader called him back.

"Wait, I have something to show you."

Curious, Wolf returned. Three Fingers reached beneath the shelves and brought out a strange object, like none Wolf had ever seen. It was made of metal, several curved strips fastened loosely together. A short chain dangled from a ring at one side of the thing. The silvery metal gleamed in the dim light of the room.

"What is it?" asked Wolf. He knew that it must be a

thing of great importance, because the trader handled it with respect.

"A trap," answered Three Fingers proudly.

"A *trap?*"

"Yes. For beaver. Fox or raccoon, too, maybe. Is it not beautiful?"

That was not exactly the impression that had struck Wolf. He was thinking that an object with so much metal must be a thing of great importance. Not an object of beauty, perhaps, but of power.

"Its medicine must be strong," he said. "How can it kill the beaver?"

"It does not kill, it catches and holds. Here, I will show you."

He knelt on the floor and placed his foot on the heavy spring, compressing it so that the jaws could open. Then very carefully, he adjusted the small parts in the center of the trap, engaging a small toggle in a notch on another part. This appeared to hold the spread jaws of the trap in an open position. The trader carefully released the pressure of his foot from the spring, and stood up.

"Do not touch it," he warned, turning to pick up a heavy stick that stood in the corner.

Wolf eyed the open trap. He did not yet understand its operation. The jaws formed a circle now, lying flat on the floor. The small interconnecting parts were near the center of the circle. He could tell that this was the critical part. The trigger and catch in one of his deadfall traps worked the same way. A carefully shaped stick engaged in a notch in another, which in turn supported a heavy log. A beaver, investigating the scent of a tiny dab of beaver musk on the trigger stick, would be caught by the log as it came crashing down. But how . . . ?

"You put the scent on a tree trunk," Three Fingers explained. "Just where the beaver cannot reach. The trap will be on the ground under it, covered with a few leaves or grass. Or in shallow water. Now, look!"

Carefully, he reached with his stick to touch the small metal plate in the center of the trap. Wolf was watching closely, but even so, he was startled when the jaws snapped shut with a loud click. The entire trap jumped into the air as if alive, rattling the chain. Wolf recoiled in alarm. It had been so quick . . . like the strike of a snake, faster than the eye can follow. The other Frenchmen were laughing at his reaction.

"*Aiee!*" he said softly. "That is sudden!"

The trap's jaws were firmly locked on the trader's stick. He knelt again and released the spring's tension to recover the stick.

"But how . . ." Wolf still did not quite understand.

"When the animal stands to sniff the scent on the tree," Three Fingers explained, "he steps on the trap."

"Ah! I see. This is powerful medicine!"

"Yes! But you will use these someday."

Wolf laughed. "No, Uncle. Not one of those!"

"Yes, my friend. Already, some of the trappers among my people are using these traps. There are few now, but next season or the winter after that . . . You can trade furs for more traps!"

"*Aiee!* I do not think so, Uncle. But thank you for showing me. I will come back next year."

"It is good! And good hunting until then."

Wolf wandered out across the meadow, to where the

big lodges of the People were coming down in preparation for travel. There was always a bit of excitement in the
air during preparation for departure. New places, new
sights and sounds, new happenings.

It would take more than half a moon, it was said, to
reach the agreed-upon site for the Sun Dance. His rival
would be with the band at least that long. Wolf hoped that
he would have a chance to talk to Rain. If, of course,
White Feathers was not hovering over her at every moment. And if he and Rain had not already made plans to
marry. It was very tempting to simply retreat, to leave the
field of conflict to avoid the hurt of a loss in such a battle
of the heart.

No, he decided, he would *not* leave the contest open to
his rival. He must be more aggressive. Even though he
was certain that White Feathers would be pushing his
courtship, playing his flute, trying to win Rain's affection,
he must at least try.

Wolf helped to take down the lodge, with the assistance
of his older brother whose lodge was nearby. Then a bit of
help for an older couple who always camped near his
parents. He finished and looked around the camp. There
were only a couple of spidery skeletons of lodge poles still
standing. Even as he watched, people were taking them
apart, a pole at a time. Now one was reduced to the last
three poles, and the three-legged bundle was toppled to
remove the last ties.

The first families were already beginning to line out on
the trail to the southwest, their horses pulling heavily
laden pole-drags. *Travois,* Three Fingers had called the
pole-drag. The traders had many new words that the People were beginning to use. *Parfleche,* the rawhide pack

carrier used by the People. *Cache* seemed a useful term, for the storage place in which they would leave supplies for a short time. Customs were changing, and so was the language of the People, though at the time the use of new words seemed of little importance.

By noon the band was out on the prairie, traveling well. The column moved in a loose single file, sometimes two or three abreast. Wolves scouted the way, some distance ahead of the main column, and other wolves rode the flanks and rear. This was primarily from custom, as no danger was likely. The People were in their own country and had few enemies. But there was vulnerability in travel, especially when the entire band was on the move, including women, children, and the old. It was unwieldy and cumbersome to transport lodge covers and poles, as well as all the worldly possessions of every family in the band. There could be no maneuverability at all, and it would take precious time even to assume a defensive position if needed.

Singing Wolf and Fast Turtle assisted with the horse herd for a while. The herd was kept bunched as a unit, although loosely, strays and stragglers urged on by the young men. The horses traveled to the right of the main column, two or three bow shots away. The prevailing south breezes made it almost mandatory for the horse herd and its inescapable dust to remain north of the main column.

Dust was not a major problem today, however. The gentle rains of the Moon of Growing had watered the prairie well. The green of the grasses, the special color that is unique to tallgrass prairie, shone at its best today. Brighter green nearby, the grasses took on a bluish cast with distance. Rolling hills a day's travel ahead seemed to blend into the same blue as that of distant sky.

After a while, one of the older men of the warrior society approached.

"Wolf," he called, "would you trade off with one of the men at the back of the column?"

"Of course, Uncle."

He reined his horse around and trotted back to the indicated position. There, one of the riders had dismounted and was examining his horse's foot. The other rider was waiting.

"*Ah-koh*, Wolf," he greeted. "We ride together today, no?"

It was White Feathers.

15

»» »» »»

It was not a comfortable situation. The last thing that Singing Wolf would have wished was an afternoon alone with his rival for the affection of Rain. He wished that his friend Fast Turtle had offered to accompany him in the duty to which he now turned. It would not have been unusual for Turtle to do so on a whim. He was pleasant, easygoing, and unpredictable. Just as easily Turtle could have said, "I will go along." Or simply reined his horse around without comment, to ride beside his friend Wolf.

But it was not so. Now Wolf rode beside White Feathers, irritation smoldering deep within him, like hardwood coals buried in ashes to save overnight. It was with resentment that Wolf looked across the grassy prairie to where the horse herd traveled. It was a few hundred paces, but he could plainly see Fast Turtle, riding with some of the other young men, laughing and joking as they rode. Sometimes a horse would try to fall behind to graze. Then one or two of the riders would pull aside to chase the errant animal back to the herd.

On such a day as this, herding the horses was more like a game than a responsibility. There was little dust, the pace was easy, and there was the occasional chance for a brief chase. Fast Turtle was having fun, which caused further resentment on the part of Wolf. Surely, any time now, Turtle would glance over and realize what an uncomfortable situation Wolf faced. He would then ride casually over to join the two scouts who brought up the rear of the column.

Even as he thought these thoughts, however, Wolf knew that it would not happen. Turtle would continue to blunder along, enjoying himself, unaware of the feelings of others. It was his way. Turtle was a good friend, and dependable in the hunt or in a fight. There was none better to ride with. But, in some ways, he could be very frustrating. Especially, Wolf thought, in the area of human emotions. Turtle should be able to *see* his discomfort and come to help. But, no, there he was, riding with the others, laughing and joking . . . *Aiee!* Had Fast Turtle ever had a serious thought?

"The day is good for travel," observed White Feathers conversationally.

"What . . . ? Oh, yes."

He did not want to talk to the man.

"Does it go well with your thunderstick?" asked White Feathers.

"Yes."

"Good. Three Fingers has taught you well?"

"Yes. I have powder and bullets now."

"It is good. The gun shoots better with the right size, no?"

"Yes, much better."

"Three Fingers was very helpful to me, too."

They rode in silence a little longer, and then White Feathers spoke again.

"When do you think we will reach the Sun Dance?"

"Who knows? Our band has never come this way before."

"Nor ours. I only wondered. I have not seen my mother and father since last season, you know."

A mixture of emotion churned in Wolf's stomach. His first thought was simple: *And that was your choice!* Close on the heels of that, however, came another, a calmer, more rational thought, one that even held a little sympathy.

"That is a long time to be away from family," he said aloud.

White Feathers glanced at him as if a little surprised.

"Yes, that is true," he said quietly.

Now Wolf was feeling sympathy for his companion, for this man that he wanted to hate and could not. This could be a good friend, he knew, except for the rivalry for Rain's affection. But now, within a moon, it seemed that the matter must reach its climax. They would be at the Sun Dance. When the ceremonies were over, the bands would again go their separate ways. If White Feathers' courtship proved unsuccessful at that time, he would probably go back to the lodge of his parents. That would be good. On the other hand, if the couple was prepared to marry, they would probably stay with the Southern band, moving in with Rain's parents. *Aiee,* Wolf did not know whether he could tolerate such a thing. Maybe he would have to leave, join another band, even.

Suddenly an idea came to him. Maybe he could find out!

"You will move back in with your parents?" Wolf asked, trying to appear casual.

There was no answer for a little while. Then White Feathers gave a deep sigh.

"I do not know," he said sadly. "Maybe so. But I have been courting, my friend. The girl called Rain. She has not given me an answer."

Wolf's head whirled with a flurry of emotions. First, joy and elation. Here was evidence that White Feathers and Rain had *not* made any plans. But the courtship was still going on, and that could change at any moment.

Closely following, though, another thought—*He does not know*—Wolf realized: *No one has told him that Rain and I have been . . .* had been *what?* He wondered. Childhood friends? Was there really ever anything else between them? He did not know what to say, what to think, even. For a moment he considered a bold move. *She has not given you an answer,* he wanted to say, *because she belongs to me!*

But that, too, was untrue. Thinking quickly, he realized that it would be to his advantage to say nothing of his own feelings for Rain. He could find out more in this way. Now if he could only think of a comment that would seem logical and not reveal too much anxiety.

His thoughts were interrupted as a rider came loping back along the column. It was apparent that the front of the procession had stopped, and the spaces were closing as the stragglers in the rear rejoined the others. There was a crackle of excitement in the air as people called to each other, questioning. The young man slid his horse to a stop.

"Broken Lance wants you two with him!" he called. "I will stay here."

"What is it?"

"The wolves in front have sighted another band."

"The Northern band, maybe," guessed Wolf.

"No. Strangers. Go!"

Strangers! A chill of excitement crept up his spine, to grip the back of his neck. With sweating palms, he reined his horse past the straggling column and kicked it into a lope. White Feathers was at his elbow.

Why could the chief possibly want us? he asked himself.

And "strangers" . . . He could not recall such an incident. Occasionally, while the band had been traveling, he remembered such encounters. Usually another band of the People. Sometimes, if they were far enough southwest, they would meet a band of Head Splitters. These were allies, and it was good. They would sometimes share a campsite for a night or two, and the tales were good around the story fires.

This was something else. An unknown.

They neared the head of the column and saw Broken Lance with a few of the band's subchiefs, clustered together and staring into the northwest. There, a few bow shots' distance away, stood a caravan much like their own. The other people, too, were milling around nervously. A cluster of their leaders had drawn aside. Wolf saw a small child toddle out into the open, and a frightened mother ran to grab him up and carry him back to the safety of the group. *They are much like us,* Wolf thought.

Now Broken Lance turned to White Feathers.

"Do you know these people, my almost-son?"

For a moment, Wolf was disgusted. The venerable band chieftain, asking advice from an upstart youngster of another band! And the *Eastern* band? It was sickening.

Then common sense came to the rescue. White Feathers *was* more likely to be familiar with other tribes using this area than anyone in the Southern band. Reluctantly, he had to agree. It was a good move on the part of Broken Lance.

"No, Uncle, I do not know them," admitted White Feathers.

At least he admits it, thought Wolf.

"And you, Curly?" asked the chief.

Wolf turned to look. He had not been aware that one of the French from the trading post had come with them. "Curly" was so called because of his hair. The hair of the People, as well as most other tribes, was usually quite straight. True, there was an occasional wavy-haired descendant of Sky-Eyes or Woodchuck, Frenchmen who had joined the People generations ago. But even that was unusual. And the hair of this man, Curly, was more tightly curled yet. Almost like that of the buffalo.

Curly shook his head. "No, my chief. I have not seen these before."

Five riders were moving at a walk, out from the other column. The right arm of the man in the center was raised, palm outward. That would be their leader.

The ceremonial meeting was quite strict at this point.

There must be no slipups, because of the vulnerability of women and children. Both groups were at equal risk, so there would likely be no skirmish. Even so, Wolf's heart quickened, and his hands were damp.

The greeting party from the other column had reached a point about halfway between the groups and stopped, waiting. Broken Lance looked around and spoke crisply, choosing those who would flank him.

"Strong Bow . . . Curly . . . White Feathers . . . Wolf. Wolf, uncase your thunderstick!"

Singing Wolf pulled off the gun's cover and handed it aside. He could hardly believe the responsibility and the honor that was being thrust upon him. But *why?* And why the others? Strong Bow, of course, a noble warrior . . . But Curly, not even of the tribe? And two very young warriors, one from the Eastern band! Had Broken Lance gone mad in his old age?

But then, as they moved forward, spread out into a rank five warriors wide, Wolf suddenly saw the reason. From the viewpoint of the strangers, here was a band led by a respected elder. Another mature warrior flanked him, and on the other side a French ally. Then the two young and active warriors, armed with . . . *Aiee,* the last three of the five were armed with thundersticks. What an impression that might make!

No, Broken Lance was far from madness. Once more he was showing the cleverness that made him a leader of the People.

16

》》》

Singing Wolf eyed the greeting party that formed a counterpart of their own. A middle-aged chief, flanked by two capable-looking warriors on each side. One was scowling fiercely, but that was probably just show. Another carried a thunderstick, the wooden stock heavily decorated with brass tacks. The effect was attractive, thought Wolf. Maybe he should ask Three Fingers about those little brass tacks next year.

He tried to identify the tribe of these strangers. The cut of their buckskins was quite similar to that of the People, but there were subtle differences. The style in which their hair was plaited, too, was unfamiliar.

Broken Lance drew his party to a halt, facing the strangers a few paces away. This was a tense moment, until a conversation was established. It is more difficult to fight a man with whom you are talking.

The two leaders exchanged greetings and Broken Lance, in his deceptively easy manner, began to sign.

"It is a good day to travel."

"Yes, a good day."

"Have you come far?"

"Today, not far. This season, yes. We come from farther north."

This was establishing several facts. Most importantly, the newcomers were skilled in hand signs, so communication would be easy.

"How are you called?" asked Broken Lance.

"We call ourselves the People," signed the other. "Others call us by other signs."

He demonstrated a hand sign or two, gestures unfamiliar to Wolf. Something about a river, which Wolf decided must refer to some river to the north.

"It is the same with us," answered Broken Lance. "We call ourselves the People. Is it not so with everyone?"

The two leaders chuckled comfortably together.

"We are sometimes called 'People of the Horse,' " Broken Lance continued, "because our people were among the first in the area to use 'elk-dogs.' "

The other man nodded.

"We thought that you might be the Horse People," he noted. "I see your young men also use thundersticks."

"Yes, we have a few."

This apparently relaxed part of the conversation was perhaps the most important, Wolf knew. Both chiefs were probing for information. The relative strength of each group was easily apparent, simply by counting numbers.

Likewise it was possible to judge their affluence and general well-being by counting horses. A large, healthy horse herd indicated a vigorous band. In this case, there seemed very little difference between the two groups. The question about the thundersticks was a probe to try to learn how well-armed the other group might be.

"We, too," answered the other chief.

It was a noncommittal answer on both sides. The newcomers could see that there were at least three such weapons in Broken Lance's band. This made the single gun in the hands of the other party less impressive. Surely, if they had more, they would have displayed them.

On the other hand, there might be the possibility that the outsiders were hiding a thunderstick or two, concealing their strength. Wolf knew that Broken Lance was probably considering this.

"Where are you going?" he asked casually.

"We are just traveling," the other man signed. "We do not wish to intrude."

"What do you seek?"

Now the important parts of the exchange were out in the open.

"We do not really know . . . milder winters, maybe. Is there a place not used by your people, where we might summer while we consider?"

This was a placating answer, designed to calm any fears of invasion. Sincere or not? It remained to be seen. Broken Lance smiled calmly.

"Yes," he agreed, "a milder winter is something we all need. Let us camp together tonight and talk of these things."

Clever, thought Wolf; Broken Lance was setting up a

situation in which they could find out more about the strangers and their motives. This, in a setting with little risk, because of the presence of the families of both sides.

"It is good," signed the other chief. "I am Long Shirt. How are you called?"

"Broken Lance."

The other nodded. "Where do you go for the summer?"

"Just now, to our Sun Dance, with the other bands of our nation. You have a Sun Dance?"

"No, but we know of them. A good tradition. Where is it held?"

This was further sparring, to gain information.

"Southwest of here. Maybe ten sleeps."

For a moment, Wolf was surprised that the chief would give such detailed information. Then he realized that there was no purpose in *not* giving it. The Sun Dance was the biggest event of the entire summer. Everyone on the plains would know its location. Besides, the newcomers had only to send out a few scouts to locate the site. With all the bands converging, their trails would be plainly marked by hundreds of hooves. The dragging lodge poles, too, marked travelers as a band on the move, not a hunting party. Hundreds of grooves scored the prairie sod in parallel stripes as far as the eye could see. An interested outsider had only to follow such a trail to the Sun Dance.

"Maybe we will go straight south for the summer," signed the leader of the other party. "Would that bother?"

"Maybe not. But let us camp now and we will talk of these things."

"It is good. Where?"

It was apparent that the strangers wanted no trouble.

Their chief kept asking for reassurance that there would be no resentment, and that they would not be intruding. His heart seemed good. Either that, or he was a very skillful liar. Broken Lance apparently thought that the way to decide was with further conversation. That was a wise course, Wolf thought. A more dynamic leader might have done it differently. But a more dynamic leader might also have started a challenge that could have shed blood by now.

Wolf was learning a great deal today. He had grown up thinking of the aging band chief as an ineffective old man. Other bands, he had thought, had leaders who were more exciting, who showed more action, more *leadership*. Today he was seeing that sometimes *inaction* is more productive. The apparently meaningless conversation in hand signs had already gotten past the initial risk that is always present in meeting strangers. Now they were on firm enough footing to camp together, which would allow even more information to be gathered. Broken Lance, then, far from being an ineffective leader, was an exceptionally clever one. Like a skilled storyteller who chooses his position, his light and shadow, the color of his background when he starts his presentation. The old chief had quietly maneuvered this situation to let his people appear at their best and strongest, well-armed and ready. He was even able to choose the strangers' campsite for tonight.

Aiee, what skill! As it now seemed, these newcomers would probably become friends and allies. The Southern band could report to the Big Council about their coming. If, instead, they proved to be enemies, Broken Lance had created a chance to learn all that could be learned of them.

"Let us camp there, by that stream," the old chief suggested. "There is water and grass for both horse herds. Our young men can keep them separated."

"It is good," answered Long Shirt. "Which side?"

"Both look good. We will take the west bank, since we are going that way in the morning."

The other nodded, talking to his companions and pointing.

"We will talk later, after we camp," signed Broken Lance, turning his horse away.

Wolf watched closely as the others turned. He noticed that Strong Bow had not moved, but was watching the other party even more closely than before. *Of course,* thought Wolf, *if there were to be treachery, now is the time!*

It seemed unlikely but, at such a time, treachery is most likely to be successful. Wolf kept his mount still until Strong Bow turned. The older warrior nodded at him in approval, and Wolf's heart was good. They reined back toward their own band.

The People were already moving in response to the hand gestures they had seen. It was apparent that they would camp beside the stream that could be seen a few bow shots away.

"The west side!" called Broken Lance to some who came out to meet the returning chief. "We camp there!"

Word quickly spread, and people hurried to find good campsites. They clattered across the shallow gravel bar, poles bouncing and water splashing, and scattered to begin the chores of the evening. The big lodges would not be raised. It was not necessary to go to such work for only one night, at least in good weather. A family campsite would be marked only by a cooking fire and piles of baggage. But a fire was essential, even if not for warmth or even for cooking. It marked a place of belonging, of *being*.

In a remarkably short time, fires began to blossom on both sides of the stream. The pungent smoke of buffalo chips drifted across the prairie, soon mingling with cooking smells as the People settled into their routine in a place that was home, at least for the night. By the time shadows began to lengthen, both bands were well-established for the night, and children of the two groups were playing together.

Children are allowed freedom from some of the restrictions imposed on adults. Their play is not burdened by such barriers as language and customs. They have a universal language of childhood which enables them to relate to other children. In a remarkably short while they are friends, and it was so here. How can a group of children take part in complicated games and contests without understanding a word of each other's tongue? Adults have forgotten, but children know.

It was that way on this exciting evening. Hand signs helped, of course, for both children and their elders. And, for both groups, those on the east and the west of the stream, there was special excitement at the possibility of new stories, tales of unknown places and things.

17

>> >> >>

It was a valuable evening, the camp with the newcomers from the north. There was little friction, because both groups had wintered well, and there was no shortage of game. With no competition for supplies, there was no necessity for any rivalry. Except, of course, in fun and games. If either band had been in destitute condition or, even worse, if *both* had been, it would have been a potentially dangerous situation. The least spark of misunderstanding might have started an inferno that would be as destructive as wildfire, and as dangerous.

As it happened, there was no such confrontation. Within a short while after campsites were selected, not only were children playing together, but young men were racing their horses and gambling on the outcome. Horses were traded, and there was much discussion over the fine points of various individual mounts.

Others, not so oriented to the horse, gambled with other games of chance. The toss of the plum stones was known to the newcomers, as well as the hidden-stick game. Women from the two groups chatted comfortably, admiring each other's domestic skills and ingenuity. Altogether, this seemed to be a very happy encounter. At least, so far.

There were two major gathering places after dark. One was the story fire, with storytellers of the two nations exchanging tales, much to the delight of the listeners. Again, they found much in common. The Creation story . . . the People had come from inside the earth through a hollow cottonwood, summoned by a deity. The visitors, too, it was found, had also originally been in the dark underground. They had laboriously climbed up the roots of a giant tree into the sunlight. It was much the same!

Their legendry, of course, included tales of the old times when animals could talk. There was much amusement over such stories as how Red Bird became red, and how Bobcat lost his tail. That one was completely different. For the strangers from the north, Bobcat's tail had been *frozen* off. The People's story told of a hunter who saw the tail protruding from Bobcat's hiding place in a hollow tree and chopped it off to decorate his bow case.

After listening for a little while, Singing Wolf decided that it might be wise to go over to the other fire. The group there was smaller, but more politically oriented. It was a council of sorts, though not very formal. The leaders of the two bands would discuss matters of common interest, and possibly points of potential conflict. There were several subchiefs from each side, the leading warriors whose opinion and advice were sought by the leaders in time of decision. Wolf's father, Walks in the Sun, sat at the right of Broken Lance. On his left was Strong Bow. Wolf wondered if Strong Bow, during his years with his wife's people, had ever encountered this nation of strangers. Maybe that was why he now sat at the chief's left hand. No, he would probably be there anyway, Wolf decided.

Someone beckoned from the fringe of the circle, and Wolf moved in that direction to sit. It was Fast Turtle, who shifted to make a place for his friend. Wolf was a little embarrassed. He had been listening to storytellers while Turtle, who was usually no deep thinker, was occupied in the more serious meeting of the bands' leaders. As Wolf sat, he glanced to his left to see who his other neighbor might be. It was White Feathers.

Now an even greater pall of embarrassment and guilt swept over him. Turtle and White Feathers must have arrived together. At least, they had been sitting together when Wolf walked in. Both young men had recognized the importance of this council, and had elected to attend, while he had been simply enjoying the storytelling. It was a bitter thing. Both Turtle, who seldom had a serious thought, and White Feathers, who was admired for his thoughtfulness, had seen this importance. *Aiee,* how could he, Wolf, have been so inattentive?

There was yet another thing that rankled and festered like a thorn under one's thumbnail. Turtle, his friend since childhood, had come to the council with his rival. Was White Feathers' intent to steal everything? His romantic interest, his friendship, his very dignity? What would be next? Glumly he thought that the only thing left was for his rival to move into the lodge of Wolf's parents. Wolf had been displaced in every other way. It was easy to think of this man as an enemy.

It was not so easy, however, when White Feathers was present. The very force of his spirit seemed to reach out and influence those around him. It was like that now.

"*Ah-koh*," whispered Feathers, as he moved to make room. "It is good, Wolf. They are just beginning to get serious."

Wolf knew that the preliminaries would have been the passing of the pipe around the circle, and the discussion of the weather, the season's game supply, campsites . . . Small talk. Then the two leaders would get down to talk of important things—areas that might have special significance, either to be favored or avoided. Ultimately, there would be a major decision tonight. It would probably be unspoken, but it would be there. When this council fire had burned low, there would be little doubt in the mind of either chief whether the other could be trusted or not. This would set the tone of the relationship between the two groups, maybe for generations to come. Would the newcomers be regarded as welcome friends or as invaders?

So far, the initial meeting had been friendly. The newcomers seemed open and honest. In the first conversation, the visiting chief had repeatedly stated that his people did not wish to intrude. He had asked permission, where they might camp, and had seemed to accept the prior rights of the People.

So far, however, there had been no suggestion as to their actual reasons for being here. Their chief had rather vaguely spoken of a desire to find easier winter camps, but was that not always a goal? Of course. Why *now?*

The conversation went on, with the visitor speaking of some of their encounters with other tribes and nations: Mandan, Pawnee, Omaha. It was noteworthy that these encounters had all been peaceful, though their purpose still seemed vague. Wolf longed to ask outright, but it was not for a minor warrior to do so. Until now, only the two principal leaders were conversing.

Finally Broken Lance seemed to approach the topic.

"How long have you been traveling?" he signed casually.

"Since Awakening Moon."

"No, not this season . . . Since you left your own homeland."

White Feathers nudged Wolf. "Yes," he whispered. "Finally, we will find out who they are!"

Wolf nodded agreement. He had been thinking along the same lines. That, too, was uncomfortable. Continually, he found not only his wishes and desires but his thoughts so close to those of White Feathers that it became more and more worrisome.

"Maybe," Wolf whispered. It bothered him to find himself continually agreeing with everything this man said or thought.

The visiting chief waited for a moment, apparently lost in thought. Then he began to sign, slowly and deliberately.

"You are asking," he stated, "if our hearts are good." He paused for a moment and then continued. "When did we leave our homeland? I do not know. My people have been moving for a long time. Many lifetimes. We have no special place, like your Sacred Hills. Maybe even your people came here from somewhere else."

"That is true," agreed Broken Lance, but the other continued.

"Our band has followed the French. We have traded with them and have been treated fairly."

Now Broken Lance interrupted.

"Are there no more French where you came from?"

"Yes, of course. But many others who trade with them, too. And the trade is bigger."

"I do not understand."

"You have seen the things they offer. Metal knives, arrow points, fire-strikers . . . thundersticks. Blankets. And other things, too. Some of you wear beaded shirts and moccasins. For these things you traded skins, no?"

Broken Lance nodded, still puzzled.

"So," the other continued, "fur skins become more valuable. More people try to trap them."

"I see," agreed Broken Lance. "Too many."

"Yes. We look now for places where fewer people trap for furs. Now, you must decide whether our hearts are good. We are too few to fight you. So, we ask your permission. If you say there is no place here, we will move on."

Wolf was impressed with the openness of the man's statement. How could one argue with such straightforward talk? Still, there was something . . .

"Wait," Broken Lance signed. "How is it that you do not have thundersticks, since you have been with the French?"

"We do have some," the other chief answered. "Not as many as some, because we are not large in number. It is easy for a powerful enemy to push us on, out of their land."

"But you showed only a gun or two!" Broken Lance signed.

The retort was simple, understandable, and in the form of a question.

"Would you enter a strange country with a show of force when you knew you were outnumbered?" he asked. "We do not want to look like invaders."

Broken Lance laughed. "I am made to think your heart is good," he signed. "Now, we wish to know more of your trapping. Our people are just beginning to trade more with the French. They were seldom in our area before. So, tell us."

The other man shrugged, as if he did not know what to say. "They have goods to trade that we need," he signed. "We catch furs and look for new places where we will not intrude."

Still that careful reassurance that had been in evidence from the first.

"You cannot go too much farther south," Broken Lance signed. "The fur is not good."

"How so?"

"Winters are too warm. Thick fur does not grow. Some of our people went too far south a few seasons ago."

That, of course, was a political reference for the benefit of his own people. Broken Lance had opposed the exploration, but an aspiring young leader had gone anyway. Wolf's father, Walks in the Sun, had accompanied the party, though he was not totally in sympathy, and he had brought home the survivors. His prestige was increased, and he was greatly respected as a holy man, even by Broken Lance. Still, such an opportunity as this for *I told them so* should not be wasted. The People understood. There were a few quiet smiles as the old chief continued. "Now, let us consider. We are but one band and cannot speak for all, even if we wished. But I have a thought. Why not come to our Sun Dance with us?"

The visiting chief was obviously startled. He sat without answering for a moment.

Wolf's thoughts were racing. What a clever suggestion! The newcomers were an unknown entity and should be watched. How better to watch them than to be with them? The main question was whether these outsiders would trap enough to interfere with the People. But there would be no trapping until winter now. In the meantime there were enough buffalo for all.

This action also had another benefit or two for Broken Lance, Wolf now realized. It would let the newcomers see the assembled strength of the People, with all bands assembled for the Sun Dance. Best of all, it would remove the responsibility for a major policy decision from the shoulders of wily old Broken Lance. Any decision now about the newcomers would be made by the Big Council.

If, of course, the strangers did accompany them. Even as that thought occurred, Wolf realized that the strangers *must* go with them. To refuse would be seen as a hostile act. *Aiee*, Broken Lance had done it again!

The other chief was now nodding his head in agreement. He, too, was clever enough to see how things stood.

"It is good," he signed.

18

>> >> >>

It was a bit more complicated for the two groups to travel together, though not much. The People were in a position to lead the way because it was their territory. The visitors followed. Both groups put out their own wolves, and the two chiefs rode together at the head of the column. Usually they were accompanied by a warrior or two from each band. It was not so much from distrust now as a sort of honor guard for the two leaders.

When the terrain permitted, the two bands sometimes traveled side by side. In those times there was much visiting and conversation in hand signs. Children, especially, crossed back and forth quite comfortably. Their small groups at play would spend some time with one family and then move to the other column for a while.

"It is good," Broken Lance observed to his counterpart. They had been watching a group of children at play during the evening halt.

"Yes," agreed the visiting chief. "May it always be so."

Wolf, who happened to be present, was impressed by this mutual display of trust and mentioned it to his father that evening.

Walks in the Sun nodded, but seemed a bit concerned. At least, preoccupied.

"What is it, Father?" asked Wolf. "Something is wrong?"

"I do not know, Wolf," the holy man said slowly. "There is something that I cannot quite understand."

"About these people, the travelers from the north?"

"Maybe. It is only a feeling. As if, maybe, my guide is trying to get my attention."

Wolf was astonished. His father rarely mentioned such things. The gifts of the spirit, the communication with one's spirit guide, were such intensely personal things . . .

Running Deer walked past just then, saw the concern in their faces, and paused.

"What is it, my husband?"

"What? Oh, nothing, Deer. Our son was saying how well our people relate to the visitors."

"Yes," answered his wife, puzzled. "Is not that true? I have thought that it is good."

"I, too," agreed Walks in the Sun. "So good . . . almost perfect. *Too good*, maybe. Something is wrong."

Wolf was startled again at such a statement from his father, usually a tolerant and trusting man.

"Can you cast the bones?" asked Running Deer.

"Maybe. I will try it, later."

Wolf had seen his father cast the bones many times. Usually it was in the privacy of their own lodge, though sometimes people were there, those to whom the ceremony was essential. But Wolf was aware that it was not a public ceremony. The presence of the curious observer would interfere with the ritual somehow. Maybe the spirits were offended by the gawking of disinterested onlookers. He must ask his father about that sometime. Later, when the time was right.

It was after dark when Walks in the Sun withdrew to the privacy of the flimsy brush shelter that they had constructed for the night camp. Wolf, who would normally have been around the story fires, or gaming with Turtle and other friends, had remained near his parents' fire tonight. He was concerned and curious about his father's odd statements earlier in the evening. If the holy man was to cast the bones, Wolf wanted to see. It had not yet occurred to him that perhaps his curiosity over such things of the spirit might be a prelude to finding his own gifts.

Firelight sparkled on the silver dangles of the Spanish bit, the elk-dog medicine of the People. Walks in the Sun often wore it ceremonially around his neck as a pendant or talisman. It had not been used in a horse's mouth for generations, but in this way, as a symbol of the coming of the horse to the People.

Now the holy man offered his mumbled prayers and unrolled the skin with its painted designs. He aligned it carefully to the directions by a glance at the Real-star. The shelter in which he sat had been constructed with its open side to the east, so he needed only to verify the position by the star. With continued prayer, he took the little rawhide box containing the bones and fetishes between his hands, offering it to the spirits of the four winds, the sky, and the earth. After a moment of shaking to mix the objects well, he rolled them out on the painted skin in a sweeping gesture.

Singing Wolf always felt a thrill at the way the bright stones, wooden carvings, and bits of bone skittered and jumped when they were cast. It was as if for a moment they took on a life of their own. Then the dancing objects came to rest, and Walks in the Sun leaned forward to study them, softly talking to himself. He touched a stone gently here, pointed to a bone there, and nodded tentatively.

Finally Wolf could stand it no longer.

"Yes, Father?" he blurted.

The holy man turned to look at his son with a puzzled frown.

"I do not know," he said. "Sometimes the bones are not clear. This time the signs are mixed."

"How so, my husband?" asked Running Deer.

He pointed to the skin.

"At first the signs all seemed good. Weather, hunting, friendship. But then I noticed a bad sign or two. Danger . . . death, maybe."

"To *us?*"

"To the People. Maybe . . . I cannot tell, Deer. It is a cloud that hangs over us."

"But then why is it mostly good?" asked Wolf.

Walks in the Sun shook his head.

"I do not know, my son. I am made to think that this is

a warning. An assurance, maybe, that we will do well, but that we must be very careful. Watch and listen."

"Is this not always true, Father?"

"Yes. But especially now. At least, that is what the bones seem to say to me."

He began to gather the small objects and return them to their rawhide box.

"Father . . . Is the danger to all of the People, or just a few?" Wolf asked.

Walks in the Sun paused thoughtfully, as if this was a question that he had overlooked. He looked at his son with an expression of pleased surprise but quickly recovered his composure. He turned and considered the skin again, as if trying to recall the location of some of the pieces. Then he nodded.

"Yes," he said quietly. "You are right. The threat is to all, but the real danger is to one or two! How did you know this, Wolf?"

"I . . . I did not, Father. That is why I asked."

"But you thought of it! It is good. Maybe the spirits are trying to get *your* attention. You must be alert to this, my son."

"How . . . ?"

His father interrupted, even as he continued to collect and pick up the scattered bones and stones.

"Only you will know how the gift is shown to you. One thing is sure: it will not be how you expected."

"But maybe I will not recognize it. Maybe it will not come. Maybe I will misuse it . . ."

His father was laughing.

"Your guide will not let you misuse it, if you listen well.

Maybe it will *not* come, but you must be ready. Relax,
Wolf! It is to be enjoyed, not feared, if the gift is offered."

"But the responsibility . . ."

His father became serious now.

"That is true. You can refuse if you fear the responsibility. But the rewards are great. Ah, what are we talking of?
You must first be *offered* the gift!"

He crawled outside the brush shelter and rose, stretch-
ing to ease his cramped muscles.

"So . . ." he summed up the previous conversation,
"let us be alert for danger to any of the People. But you
must also be listening if your guide calls."

Wolf did not answer. He was thinking longingly of his
childhood days in the Rabbit Society, with his friends
Rain and Fast Turtle. How simple things had seemed
then! They had played, as play is the work of children,
learning by imitating, building small lodges, and learning
the use of small tools and weapons. There had seemed to
be few worries then. None that could not be cured by an
understanding parent or other adult. Friendships were
simple and unchanging, except for minor quarrels about
minor things, forgotten before Sun Boy carried his torch
beyond earth's rim. Sometimes he longed to run back into
those easier times.

But it could not be. He was grown now. An adult, with
the responsibilities of adults. He was not yet responsible
for his own lodge, he reminded himself with a pang of
hurt as he did so. That was a responsibility that he had
looked forward to sharing with Rain. But now . . . *Aiee*,
he did not want to think of it!

In addition to all of the hurt that had burdened him, his
father had laid yet another worry on his young shoulders.

No, *two!* There was danger to the People, a danger that few realized. He must watch carefully for that. Was it somehow connected with these friendly strangers, who seemed so like the People? Apparently Walks in the Sun thought so. Besides that worry, even, was the other, vaguely suggested by his father. Was he, Wolf, to be offered the gifts of the spirits? Was it intended that he follow in his father's steps as a holy man? He had hardly considered it. He had been concerned only with the activities of a young man: hunting, horses, skills of the warrior . . .

And, naturally, girls. In his case, one girl . . . Rain. The two of them had played as children that they were setting up their lodge together. It had been an accepted fact. They had not even needed to talk of it, it seemed so easy to accept.

Until, of course, the coming of White Feathers with his sweet ways and his cursed courting flute. That was the beginning of Wolf's troubles, he thought. Life was good until then. The thunderstick . . . well, *that* was brought by Feathers, and *it* was good. In fact, White Feathers had been quite helpful to him, in learning about the new weapon. That was part of the problem. He wanted badly to hate the young man from the Eastern band but could not really do so. White Feathers was pleasant, quick in conversation, helpful, and had a good sense of humor. There was nothing about the man to dislike. And, of course, he had saved Wolf's life. What a debt! *But for that,* Wolf thought, *I should give up my woman, my almost-wife?*

But Rain had made it quite clear. She was *not* his woman until she said so. How could he worry about other dangers, or about anything, with that gray cloud bank hanging over him?

Frustrated, he climbed the little rise behind the camp to be alone. The night was warm and clear, the stars bright above him. Below, the scattered campfires of the two bands spread across the valley. They were close, yet separate. Maybe that was significant, he thought. Near, yet so far . . . He shook his head. Was he trying to see some sort of pattern in *everything*?

A flash of motion caught his eye, and he turned to watch a falling star arch across the blackness of the sky, to flicker out before it reached the earth. A sign? Maybe. Good or bad? He had no idea. It had come from the northeast and had appeared to cross over both camps below. Surely a sign. He would ask his father . . . *No!* He would try to reason it out for himself.

He looked back to the east from where the shooting star had come and realized that the moon was rising. Its blood-red rim was just creeping over the horizon. Was that, too, a sign?

19
》》》

"Come, let us hunt and try your new thunder-stick," suggested White Feathers.

Wolf was not immediately pleased with the idea. There had been no unpleasantness between them. The visitor continued to impress everyone with his generosity, good humor, and overall honesty. But to Wolf, it was almost repulsive that the young man became more and more popular. Feathers had continued his light, flirtatious courtship as they traveled, and Rain seemed to respond as blindly and happily as any of the rest to the charm of this outstanding young man.

It was because of this that Wolf hated to be in the presence of his rival. He could hardly stand to look at White Feathers, the handsome face and athletic build.

His heart was heavy as he pictured his childhood sweetheart clasped in those muscular arms, smiling, responding to the caresses . . . *Aiee*, it was too much! It made him feel inferior, lesser than the handsome visitor. He did not like the feeling; another reason to avoid the company of White Feathers.

Then he remembered his resolve, as he had reasoned it out much earlier. Every bit of time during the journey that Feathers was occupied with something else, he would *not* be courting Rain. So, if the two went hunting, it would accomplish that.

"It is good," he agreed. "But maybe we should ask."

The People were just breaking camp, and the two walked over to the campfire of Broken Lance.

"Uncle, we would ask of you," White Feathers began.

Irritation rankled in Wolf's stomach. He, Wolf, should have been the one to approach the chief. It was proper, of course, to ask permission to leave the traveling band for any purpose. The leaders must know the size and location of the band's strength in case of emergency. The availability of each warrior's skills was important to all. But the one to approach the band chief with their proposal should have been Wolf, a member of the band, not White Feathers, an outsider. Yet old Broken Lance seemed not to notice. He and his wife had so completely taken this young man into their lodge and their hearts that this breach of custom must seem logical.

"Yes, what is it, my almost-son?" Broken Lance inquired, smiling.

Wolf could stand it no longer.

"We would hunt ahead of the column today, Uncle," he blurted. "The People could use fresh meat."

The chief seemed only mildly surprised at Wolf's intrusion into the conversation.

"How many?" he asked.

The two young men looked at each other. They had not spoken of this.

"Just we two," said White Feathers. "Maybe Fast Turtle."

Again, the little twinge of resentment. White Feathers was trying to take not only his intended wife, but his friends.

"Only a small party," he agreed tightly.

Broken Lance studied them for a moment and seemed about to ask a question. Then he shrugged and nodded.

"It is good. You go straight ahead of us?"

"Yes, Uncle," answered White Feathers.

"Good. We do not want to slow the travel. If your kill is too far aside . . . Well, you both know."

They nodded and went to find their horses. Wolf explained to his parents, who wished them good hunting. He looked around for Fast Turtle, to prevent being alone all day with his rival, but could not find him. Undeserved anger flared for a moment at Turtle's absence, but Wolf quickly realized that such a reaction was ridiculous. Turtle could do as he wished.

He swung to the saddle and turned toward the agreed meeting place with White Feathers. As he threaded his way among the campfires, a movement caught his eye and he turned to look.

Why one movement should have drawn his attention, amid all the hustle and bustle of breaking camp, he was unsure. Maybe he had been looking for her. Or maybe it

was just an accident. Maybe, even, she had caused the
encounter to happen.

"*Ak-koh*, Wolf," greeted Rain. "I have not seen you
very much. How is it with you?"

Maybe, he thought, *she is looking for White Feathers.*
His throat was dry.

"I have been busy," he said, trying to appear calm. She
looked so beautiful this morning, the golden rays of the
rising sun painting her cheeks and the little dimple in her
chin . . . He shook himself mentally. "It is good with
me," he went on stiffly. "And you?"

He hated, almost, to ask that. The terrible thought
flashed through his mind that she would tell him: *Yes, it is
wonderful, and I am to marry White Feathers at the Sun
Dance camp.*

But she did not say that. She looked at him for a little
longer, seemingly as embarrassed as he was. Finally she
spoke again, gesturing at his horse and the gun across his
saddle.

"You are a wolf today?"

It was small talk, a conversation to break the awkward
silence.

"No," he said, "a hunter. There is need for meat."

"Alone?" she asked. It was still just small talk. "Or with
Fast Turtle?"

That was a logical question, and it was purely by accident that it trod on his toes. His most sensitive toes, in
fact. He reddened.

"No," he blurted, "with White Feathers."

Now the girl reddened. "Ah!" she said, her voice tense.
"I see . . . I . . . It is . . . Well, good hunting!"

She turned and almost ran from the scene. Wolf,

equally upset, yanked his horse around and rode to meet his rival.

The two rode southwest, ahead of any others, scouting for game. It would be better, of course, not to make a major kill, such as elk or buffalo, until nearer the place where the caravan would stop for the night. If they found game immediately, it would not be a very welcome kill. The entire band must stop and wait while the butchering proceeded. That, or a few must stay behind, virtually unprotected. Ideally, they would make their kill in mid-to-late afternoon, near a favorable campsite. As the old joke went, "Drop the meat beside the cooking fire."

So, it would be most of the day that they would ride together. They looked back, to see the twin columns beginning to form up in the valley behind them. Wolves were being posted, pole-drags assembled, baggage loaded. The horse handlers were rounding up strays. It was a good feeling, to be a part of such a band. Of such a nation as the People.

But just now, there were other considerations. It would be better to put some distance between them. The hunters would ride well ahead and begin their serious hunting nearer the evening's halt. With this in mind, they kicked the horses into an easy lope, covering ground yet not pushing too hard. Alternately, they would pull in to a walk, letting the horses blow for a while. Occasionally, they would even halt to let the horses graze while the hunters walked around to ease tired muscles.

They bypassed several small bands of grazing buffalo. It was a good sign to see the scattered animals, eagerly grazing the new growth. If they could find such a band this afternoon, near grass and water . . . A fat yearling, maybe.

It was during one of the stops to rest men and horses that they began a serious conversation. White Feathers initiated it with no warning, as they discussed their weapons and the coming hunt.

"You have not fired your gun anymore?" White Feathers asked.

"No. There has been no chance."

He knows that, thought Wolf irritably. Any shot fired within some distance of the traveling column would have been heard by all. There had been none.

"It would be good to practice," suggested Feathers. "It is like learning the use of the bow. You hit nothing at first."

Wolf smoldered with anger.

"I do not want to waste my powder and lead," he snapped irritably.

"*Aiee!* That is not a waste, it is a saving!" protested White Feathers. "You will make more shots count when they must!"

"My shots will count. You think of your own!"

It was an angry retort, one that was unjustified. Wolf knew it but did not care. He was reaching the end of his rope. He stopped and was quiet, embarrassed by his outburst but still angry. White Feathers, too, was quiet for a little while. It was he who finally broke the uncomfortable silence.

"Wolf," he said slowly, "I am made to think that your heart is not good toward me. I do not understand. I have wished to be your friend. I have tried to help you with your thunderstick, but you did not want it. What is it?"

Wolf sat quietly for a moment, lost for an answer. He could not say his real reasons, his jealousy over Rain or his frustration at owing his life to his rival. If the man were only a bit less assured and confident. But now White Feathers was continuing.

"I try to make myself pleasant and helpful," Feathers went on thoughtfully. "It is not easy to come here to your people, a joke from the Eastern band."

"Wh-what?" stammered Wolf.

"Of course you know nothing of what I feel," White Feathers was saying. "You have always had it all. Sure of yourself, confident, admired by others . . ."

"*Aiee!*" gasped the startled Wolf. "I have thought the same of you. I was jealous of you because . . ." He paused. This was perilously close to his real reasons for dislike . . . "Because you are so admired and well-liked."

Now White Feathers was laughing.

"It is good!" he chortled. "Is there any reason we should not be friends then?" He paused, watching Wolf's face closely. "There is!" he stated, becoming serious. "What is it, Wolf?"

"No, we *are* friends," insisted Wolf. "But . . ." *Well, why not get everything out in the open?* he thought. "My heart is heavy over your courting Rain."

"Rain?" gasped White Feathers. "*You?*"

"You did not know? We have been close since childhood!"

It felt good to get this out.

"But why did someone not tell me? Fast Turtle?" White Feathers asked.

"Who knows? Turtle . . ."

"Yes, I understand. Turtle is my friend, too!"

Both chuckled.

"But . . . why has Rain allowed me to court her?"

That was a very uncomfortable question. Because she was angry? No, that would not do.

"Well, we had not yet made plans to marry . . . We . . ." Wolf stammered.

"Then she is single? She *can* be courted?"

It was bitter in his mouth, as the realization finally came to him.

"It must be her choice," Wolf admitted.

"Good. Then it should not stand between us?"

"Well, no . . ."

But both knew that it did.

20

>> >> >>

Rain had seen the two men ride out as the camp prepared to move that morning. She watched them grow smaller in the distance and finally disappear over the rise to the southwest. It might be a cause for concern.

At first she had thought that maybe they were to ride as wolves. That gave her a sense of pride, that warriors so young would be chosen for the important place in front of the column. But this appeared to be something else. The two continued straight on, beyond the usual range of scouts, on out of sight. This must be something special. Rain longed to inquire but was reluctant to do so. She was unsure in her own mind how she felt about these two. Her family and friends were watching for any sign, teasing occasionally. Any inquiry on her part, however slight, would start another round of jokes and questions as to which suitor she would choose. And she had no ready answer.

There was still a pang of hurt when she thought of her quarrel with Singing Wolf. He was her lifelong friend, the one with whom she had always imagined spending her life. They would set up their lodge together, raise their children. She would help him.

Rain had always suspected that Singing Wolf would probably follow the vocation of his father. She knew from childhood that Wolf already had many of the gifts of the spirit. He would watch two birds, sitting in the top of a distant dead tree, silhouetted against the sunset. It was a game, sometimes a wager, with a couple of the boys placing bets on which bird would fly first. Wolf was always right, able to know before they flew. He never placed bets on it. He had once told her that it would not be fair.

It was possible that an acute observer could tell which bird seemed the most restless and predict its departure. Rain did not think it was so with Singing Wolf. He was observant, yes. But this was a different sort of gift. He was *always* right, not merely most of the time.

Not only the birds . . . He could also predict such things as the toss of the plum stones. That was an ever-popular game for all ages. Any odd number of plum stones could be used, usually five or seven. After they were dried, one side would be painted red. When they were shaken and tossed on the ground or on a skin spread between the players, some would land with the red side up, others showing the natural yellow. Players would sometimes bet large amounts on a single roll.

Singing Wolf never wagered on the plum stones. He

never said much about it. Yet, Rain had come to the con-
clusion quite early that there was a reason. It must be like
the birds in the tree, she thought. Wolf must *know* how
the roll of the plum stones would be. Therefore, like the
wager on the birds' flight, it would for Wolf be "unfair."

She had spent a lot of thought about this during their
years of growing-up in the Rabbit Society. It was well
known that any gift of the spirit must be used properly
and ethically. Misuse would result, at the very least, in the
loss of the gift. At worst, it could be fatal. A holy man, for
instance, using the power of his medicine for personal
revenge or gain would surely die.

Rain had often watched her friend with his minor gifts
of insight with awe and wonder. He never said much
about it. It was something that was just there. But there
seemed to be rules that he followed. Maybe they were
given *with* the gift . . . what would be "fair," what
would be misuse. She had been close to Wolf long enough
and closely enough to see some of the rules. He would not
use these powers of insight for personal gain. That was
why he would not gamble.

She was not certain that Wolf understood this completely. Sometimes she thought she knew him better than
he did himself. Her childhood fantasies had always included the two of them, growing up and establishing their
own lodge. Wolf would follow in the footsteps of his father, receiving the powerful spirit-gifts as he matured. He
would become the wearer of the elk-dog medicine, the
Spanish bit that allowed the People to control the horse.

And she would help him in all ways. Not only in establishing a lodge befitting the prestige of a respected holy
man. Not only bearing his children. The duties of a holy

man's wife were filled with responsibility. As Running
Deer now did for her husband, Rain would learn to identify, gather, and prepare the medicine plants. She must
learn the ceremonies, the chants and songs, and would
probably be given the honored task of sounding the cadence on the drum while he sang.

It was an exciting fantasy, one she had treasured for
years. That was not to deny that there were diversions, of
course. She had sometimes imagined other choices for
herself. One of her other fantasies was that she would be
a warrior, like her ancestor Running Eagle. The exploits
of that great warrior woman were still recounted in legend
and song. But, mostly, her dreams and plans were with
Singing Wolf.

It had been a pleasant diversion the previous season,
when the young men of the Eastern band had joined
them for the summer. It was stimulating and exciting, and
the most handsome of them, White Feathers, had obviously taken great interest in her. There was something
about the birdlike tones of the courting flute that made
her skin tingle. Feathers was an able hunter and warrior,
too, it seemed. She was pleased when the young man was
invited to stay in the lodge of the band chief for the season. Pleased and proud, maybe, that such a man was interested in courting *her*.

This led to another fantasy, one completely new. In this
scenario, she would be courted avidly by this handsome
and respected man. At the proper time, they would
marry. Her father would spread the blanket over the
shoulders of the couple, symbolizing that they were now
one. Then she and White Feathers would establish their

lodge together. He would join the Southern band, and they would raise beautiful children.

Rain had really not considered this fantasy any more than that, an amusing possibility. A diversion, maybe. An amusing story for her grandchildren. The grandchildren that she would have with Singing Wolf.

That had all changed quite suddenly when she and Wolf quarreled. Actually, she had at one time considered sharing with him her thoughts about White Feathers. That would assure Wolf that the courtship was not really serious, merely a diversion. Wolf would probably say very little, but would smile, his gentle smile of amusement. Then they would chuckle together over the thought that anyone could ever come between them.

Then Singing Wolf . . . *Aiee,* how could he have been so stupid? She still became angry at the thought. He had actually forbidden her to be interested in the handsome young visitor. She had become angry, and then his jealous rage flared up. They had hardly spoken since, beyond a passing greeting.

White Feathers had, from time to time, come courting. Rain was sure that soon he would push her for a decision. Probably he would want to make the announcement at the Sun Dance, when all the bands were together and his people were there. That time was drawing closer, only a few days now, half a moon at most. It was a bit frightening. She concentrated on the fantasy in which she and her handsome husband became one of the most admired and respected couples in the Southern band. Their fine lodge, their beautiful children.

Sometimes she thought of Wolf with a pang of remorse. What might have been . . . Then her anger would rise again, and she would remind herself that their quarrel was Wolf's fault. The destruction of their shared fantasy was his doing. Her anger at him helped to feed her other fantasy and to justify it. She would show him, and he would regret the day that he tried to tell *her* what she must do or not do.

She tried to crowd out the thought that she, too, regretted that day. That thought irritated her considerably each time it surfaced. She tried to shove it back out of sight, to ignore it, but that was only partially successful.

It irritated her that she had so far been unable to tell White Feathers about her lifelong friendship with Singing Wolf. That they had been on the verge of marriage . . . Should it not be pleasant to mention with amusement the failure of another suitor? She did not even know whether White Feathers knew of that long friendship. It was not that she wanted to keep it from him, exactly. Surely he knew. He had become friends with Fast Turtle, and Turtle . . . But wait! Turtle was a strange one. He might deliberately avoid the subject so that he could enjoy watching the developments. No. Turtle was not that smart. Probably he had been so busy and preoccupied with his own interests that it had not even occurred to him to talk of the romances of others.

But today Rain was startled to see her two suitors riding off together. She knew that they had talked, at least some. The thundersticks. These two both possessed thundersticks. She was certain that White Feathers had assisted the instruction of Wolf in the weapon's use. That must have been a bitter taste for Wolf. She smiled at the thought. He deserved it! Yet there was a sorrow, too. She found herself hurting for him.

The question still nagged at her, however: *What are they doing together?* Was this some sort of warrior thing, that they intended to fight each other to establish a right to her lodge? That was an exciting thought, but she was immediately ashamed of it.

Closely following came another, an alarming thought. Both were well-armed, well-mounted . . . *Aiee*, both carried thundersticks! Was it possible that they would do such a thing as that which now crossed her mind? At first she had been thinking in terms of a contest, each showing his skills. But they could have done that in the presence of everyone. Why would they leave the caravan? Could it be that they would find a private place and let the thundersticks decide at a distance? She could visualize the two, firing until only one still stood.

She dreaded the coming of evening, yet the day seemed so long ahead. There was no one with whom she could share her fears. She must live with it today, and at the day's end see whether one man or two rejoined the camp.

And if only one, *which one?*

21

» » »

The two men stood still, listening for the cry to be repeated. They heard the expected sounds of the insects, the chortling warble of the yellow-breasted lark. High overhead, a hawk screamed shrilly. But there was nothing else, no sound except the song of the breeze through last season's dried prairie grasses.

"Was there not a horse?" asked White Feathers.

"I thought so, too," Wolf answered. "But where?"

They had dismounted for a short rest before crossing the steep ridge ahead. Beyond, Wolf knew, lay a long flat valley. It would be quite likely to have buffalo grazing along the wandering stream's floodplain. There the soil was deep and rich and the grasses lush.

They had just been ready to remount when a horse

sounded a long whinnying call. Instantly both men placed hands over the noses of their own mounts to prevent them from answering. A horse's call was not unusual, or even alarming in most situations. But here and now, it must be considered. They were not aware of any other horsemen in the area, and the source of the cry must be identified. Though there were no known enemies, that possibility was not entirely out of the question.

More likely, another hunter or party of hunters were also seeking meat. If not from their own band, it could be hunters from one of the other bands that were now converging for the Sun Dance. Even the Growers sometimes hunted for meat when conditions were favorable. Wolf was not familiar enough with the area to be sure whether there were Grower villages here, but it was a likely possibility. None of these situations would actually be dangerous, but it was a matter of etiquette. To blunder into the hunt of someone else would be an absolute taboo. They must, before all else, be certain who was in the area and what they were doing. At best, it was the polite thing to do. At worst, a wrong guess could be fatal if unknown strangers were present.

The cry was not repeated, and the two began to relax.

"Did we really hear it?" White Feathers asked softly.

"I think so. Maybe beyond the ridge? It was some distance away."

"Yes. Do you get the feeling that there is a herd, a big herd, in the valley beyond the ridge?"

Wolf nodded. There was a *feel* about it, maybe the low mutter of a multitude of grazing animals, not quite audible but felt as a background noise. Like the purr of distant thunder, maybe, in a summer storm seen only as a thin blue cloudbank a day's travel to the southwest. Possibly there were vibrations through the earth itself, in response to the weight of thousands of sharp black hooves on the deep-rooted sod.

"Maybe it is a herd of horses," suggested Wolf.

White Feathers nodded. "Maybe. But we must know."

"That is true."

Even if the valley was filled with horses, it did not answer all of the questions. Wild horses? Or the horse herd of a large group of traveling strangers? Their course of action would be entirely different, depending on which situation proved correct. A wild horse hunt would be a pleasant diversion that could result in the capture of valuable animals. If it proved to be the herd of a group of travelers, that would be another matter.

"We have to look over the ridge," Wolf went on. "But let us be cautious. Look, we can leave the horses here. You go to the left, there, I will go up this gully to the right, and we can take a look. Then meet back here to plan. It is probably buffalo anyway, and we can decide how to make our kills."

"It is good!"

White Feathers was already tying a thong around his horse's nose to prevent its whinnying. After Wolf had done the same, they decided to tie the horses, rather than allow them to graze. If there did prove to be strangers in the area, it might be necessary to find them quickly. They tied their respective mounts close together in a thicket of sumac, then separated and began the climb. A succession of shallow gullies scarred the smooth roll of the long ridge. They were a few bow shots apart, and each rose toward the summit as a dry wash. Sometimes they held a few scraggly trees and bushes, growing among the rocks.

Wolf struggled upward, panting with the exertion. It was not a hard climb, but a long slope. He paused a moment to catch his breath and glanced upward at the shelf of rimrock above him. He would not be able to climb over the shelf but must leave the gully soon to find a better path. A little farther . . .

He stopped suddenly in mid-stride, listening. There had been a sound close ahead of him in the gully. A dull clumping sound, the unmistakable stamp of a horse's front foot as it fights the nuisance of flies. Wolf crouched against the rocks and looked quickly around. He felt very foolish. He had not been alert. An enemy could easily have ambushed him. There was nothing else, no sound, no sign of anyone. He moved forward, placing his feet carefully, his gun in his left hand but his throwing ax ready in his right. If he were attacked, there would be no time to ready the thunderstick.

Now he saw the horse, cleverly concealed in a little pocket under the shelf of limestone rimrock. It was tethered securely, and its muzzle was tied as he had done with his own mount. The attitude of the horse, lazing drowsily with one hind foot cocked, told that its rider was not present.

It sensed Wolf's presence and turned its head toward him, ears erect and curious. After another reassuring look around, he approached the animal. From the tracks and the absence of droppings, he determined that it had been here only a short while. This must be the animal that had called, before the rider muzzled it.

But where was that rider now? If his intentions were

honorable, why was he being so secretive? Close on that thought came the realization that the unseen stranger's actions were no different than his own. Still, a small voice of caution whispered to him in the dim corners of his mind. He must make his companion aware of the presence of the stranger.

Hurrying, but with more caution now, Wolf climbed out of his gully and moved toward the similar wash where he knew White Feathers was climbing the slope. He must get high enough to see the other man, yet try to avoid being seen himself.

A large square block of stone lay just ahead of him. Maybe he could risk climbing up on that vantage point for a few moments. It was about twice the height of a man on each side, and about the same in height. But on one side, a jumble of blocks which had fallen away from the main stone provided steps to the top. Quickly he mounted and looked around from his new vantage point.

He saw the intruder before he saw his companion. The man was two or three bow shots away, crouching and watching the gully beyond, the one up which White Feathers was climbing. It was not a good situation.

He started to shout, and then realized that this would warn the stranger, whose motives were still unclear. Wolf decided to watch for a little longer. Almost immediately he saw White Feathers advance up the furrowed slope. Wolf could see him only from the waist up, but he was sure that the man in hiding would have a much better view. In fact . . . another twenty paces or so would bring White Feathers into an area where the gully flattened out. There was no protection at all for a few steps . . .

Wolf was already preparing his thunderstick, checking

the priming in the pan. He was not sure yet, but it seemed that . . . Yes! The stranger was now cautiously rising to one knee, fitting an arrow to the bowstring. It must be his plan to kill White Feathers as he reached the place of no protection.

An evil thought flitted through his mind. If that happened, it would solve many of the problems that he now faced. Instantly, it was gone, and he was about to rise and shout a warning. Then another idea made itself felt. Before it had hardly solidified he was raising the thunderstick, pulling back the flint, and leveling the muzzle at the distant assassin. Even if he missed, the shot would warn White Feathers.

The gun boomed, and his vision was obscured for a moment by the puff of cottony white smoke. Anxiously, Wolf peered forward, even as he began to reload. The smoke thinned, and he saw that he had not missed. The would-be assassin lay sprawled facedown, his bow under him. White Feathers was crouched behind a boulder, gun ready.

Wolf glanced around, looking for any other enemies, but saw none. He stood and waved to White Feathers, then finished reloading, climbed down, and sprinted in that direction. His companion was just approaching the still figure on the ground, alert for any sign of life.

"You saved my life," said White Feathers shakily.

"I only repaid a debt," Wolf answered. "Who is he?"

They rolled the man over, his sightless eyes staring into the sky.

"*Aiee,*" White Feathers exclaimed. "Do we not know this man?"

"Yes! One of the strangers who travels with us, is it not? But why . . . ?"

"It is! Remember, he was in the greeting party! Did you see anyone else?"

"No. I found his horse. This is a very strange thing," Wolf answered.

"This is the one who glared at us, no?"

"Yes, maybe so. They all look much alike. But, come, let us look around. We must be sure there are no more."

By unspoken consent they stayed together now, climbing the short distance to the top of the ridge. In the valley below were large numbers of quietly grazing buffalo, undisturbed by the echoing shot.

"I am made to think," said Wolf quietly, "that we should leave them alone until we are sure about this other thing."

White Feathers nodded. "It is good. But we must be careful, too. Maybe there are more. What shall we do with him?"

"Take him back, I guess. I have his horse, over there."

"It is good. But we need not go too far. They are coming this way, no?"

"Yes." Wolf glanced at the sun. "We should see them before long." He paused. "Wait! What if the strangers have started trouble as they travel?"

The two looked at each other for a moment, and then White Feathers spoke.

"It is best that we go back to meet them. Let us leave this man and his horse."

They turned to hurry down toward their horses.

22

»» »» »»

On the way back to rejoin the main party the two discussed how they should present their news. They had carried the body of the dead warrior over to the gully where the horse was hidden and concealed it there. The horse was unsaddled and turned loose to graze. Almost as an afterthought they rode down into the valley far enough to shoot two fat yearlings. This would satisfy their mission.

They decided to relay their startling news very quietly. It was a delicate situation. If they rode in shouting their tale of treachery, it could ignite bloodshed beyond all imagination.

It was not long until they saw the double column approaching. Everything seemed quiet and orderly. They visited with the advance wolves for a moment and told of their buffalo kills.

"Ah! It is good!" chortled one of the scouts. "My stomach speaks even now for broiled hump ribs."

They did not mention their more serious experience, having decided to take that news directly to the leaders. The two joined the small party in the lead where the chiefs rode.

"*Ah-koh*, my chief," greeted White Feathers. "We have had good hunting. There is meat tonight!"

Wolf found that he no longer resented this direct approach by White Feathers. The importance of their mission now overshadowed such petty feelings. He was watching the visiting chieftain closely, but there was no sign of anything amiss.

"We have meat," Wolf signed to the visitors.

"It is good!" the chief signed back.

Now, how to approach the leaders of the People without letting these others know? It was uncertain whether they had picked up enough of the language of the People to follow such a conversation. The riders who formed the honor guard for Broken Lance were Strong Bow and Walks in the Sun, and an idea struck Wolf.

"May we ride with you a little way, Uncle?" he asked Broken Lance. "I would speak with my father."

"Of course, my son," the old chief agreed.

Wolf caught the eye of White Feathers, who nodded agreement. He reined in beside his father.

"It goes well with you, Father?" he asked conversationally.

"Of course. What is it, Wolf?" asked Walks in the Sun, puzzled.

"Come aside a little," Wolf spoke quietly. "We need your counsel."

His father reined imperceptibly away from the chief, and White Feathers drifted into the space created. *It is good,* thought Wolf, motioning to his father to come farther aside.

When they were a little distance away, Walks in the Sun could wait no longer.

"What is the matter, Wolf? Something is wrong?"

"Very wrong, Father," Wolf began. "But let us look as if we are laughing and joking."

He threw his head back and chuckled, even as he began to quickly tell his grim story. To any casual observer, this was only a father and son, visiting and making small talk as they rode.

". . . so we hid the body, made our buffalo kill, and hurried back," Wolf finished. "We were afraid that it might be part of a plot of some kind."

"You have done well," his father said thoughtfully. "This is strange, Wolf. You saw no one else?"

"No."

"All seems friendship here. Now we must find a way to tell the chief." He thought for a moment. "Where is your buffalo kill?"

"Just beyond the ridge, there. It is a big valley, good for a camp."

"Yes, I know the place. Now, I want you to very quietly tell some of the warriors, so there can be no surprise. Your brother, some of his friends, maybe. I am made to think this is *not* treachery, but we must be ready. I will find a way to tell Broken Lance."

"It is good," agreed Wolf, turning his horse aside and starting back along the column.

"Your brother rides wolf to the left today," Walks in the Sun called.

Singing Wolf nodded and waved as he rode away.

Looking back later, it seemed impossible that it had gone so smoothly. It was not until after dark that the tragic events came completely into the open.

The two chiefs were seated around an evening fire, stomachs comfortably full, sharing a pipe. Both were flanked by subchiefs and advisers, likewise relaxed and comfortable. At least, to all appearances. To one who was informed, it was apparent that the men of the People were well-armed, alert and ready. It was thought that Broken Lance would introduce the conflict that lay so heavily over the camp.

"My heart is heavy this night," the old man finally signed.

"How so?" signed the other. "Can it be heavy after such a feast, and a smoke with friends?"

He seemed completely relaxed and without guile.

"It is this way," Broken Lance signed, slowly and deliberately. "Our young men were attacked today by one of yours. They killed him."

The startled look on the face of the other chief was either one of complete surprise, or a superb job of pretending, Wolf thought. This was the moment of truth. Hands tightened on weapons around both sides of the fire. The chief turned with quick questions in his own tongue, holding his right hand up in the sign of peace even as he did so. Most of his warriors shook their heads, but then one answered at length. He listened, nodding from time to time. Finally he turned back to Broken Lance.

"Brown Bear," he signed. "I am told that he left before daylight. He has not returned." He paused for a moment and then continued to sign. "Our hearts are good, my brother. I want you to know this. But we have foolish young men, as you do, maybe. This was a bad one, a troublemaker, but a fierce fighter. Your hunters were not hurt?"

"No. They were fortunate."

"Then it is good. His death is on himself."

This is too easy, thought Wolf.

"Can your warriors be trusted?" Broken Lance was signing.

"Yes, my brother. Look, we do not want trouble with our women and children here."

"Nor do we," Broken Lance answered.

The other chief sat still for a little while, as the air fairly crackled with the tension. Any little spark . . .

"Let me tell you all," the chief began again. "We have been moving because of fierce neighbors. We are tired of fighting. Maybe we could find somewhere that we did not have to fight. But we were prepared to fight if we had to. Then we met you. We have met well. Still, some wanted to show strength, though our Council decided that we would be friends and allies. Brown Bear was one who wished to fight." He paused, looked around the circle, and then continued: "My heart, too, is heavy, over the foolishness of one of us. Tell us where to find his body to care for it, and we will be gone from your country."

Wolf felt sorry for the man, who appeared to be a good

leader, betrayed by his own. There was, of course, another possibility.

"No, stay with us," Broken Lance was signing. "Come with us to our Sun Dance, as we have said."

Clever, thought Wolf. If the two groups parted, it would be more difficult to watch them. To invite them to continue to the Sun Dance was to keep them under observation. It would also prevent the warriors of the other group from returning in a sneak attack.

"I am made to believe that your hearts are good," Broken Lance went on. "But now you must prove it."

"It is good," signed the other. "I ask only such a chance."

There was some distrust as they moved on the next morning. It was still a dangerous situation. It had helped, however, that White Feathers and Singing Wolf not only showed where they had placed the body of Brown Bear, but helped prepare him for burial. He had been a loner, with no relatives and few close friends, it was said.

"He was always a little crazy," one of the young warriors told Wolf.

They placed him on a scaffold with his weapons, ceremonially broken, and returned to the camp to prepare for travel the next day. Only one day had been lost.

"We will still be there before the Eastern band," someone said.

Even White Feathers laughed, but Wolf knew that there was hurt in his heart. The joke was at his expense, and that of his people.

It was three days later that the wolves passed the word back along the column that a party of armed riders was approaching. Of course, everyone was interested in preparing for any challenge. Even more important was to watch the strangers who were traveling with them for any sign of treachery. There seemed to be none, the warriors taking only appropriate action to ready their weapons.

The newcomers, when they arrived at an easily visible distance, spread out in a line and advanced, about twenty warriors strong. It was a tense moment, especially for people who had been living with the tension of distrust.

Now the approaching warriors increased their speed to a trot, and men of the People began to move forward to meet the threat. Surely no one would try a direct charge.

Then came the war cry, a full-throated challenge from the approaching riders. A shout of recognition was relayed back down the column.

"It is our Northern band!"

"Tell our visitors! These are our own people!"

In a few moments the mock charge swept past, riders from the column circling, joining the newcomers. Yells, laughter, recognition of friends and relatives, the beginning of the exuberance of the entire Sun Dance celebration.

There were many questions and answers flying back and forth as the riders drew down to a walk. Wolf found himself riding beside a man about his own age.

"How far to the Sun Dance?" he asked.

"One sleep. Who is with you?"

"Strangers from the northeast somewhere. Their tongue is strange, but they use hand signs. Which bands are here so far?"

"Ours . . . Northern. Red Rocks. A few Head Splitters, like always. The Mountain band is yet to come. And

Eastern not here yet, of course. We thought that was who you were. Have you seen them?"

"No. We came this northern way to trade with the French."

"Ah, I see. You have a thunderstick or two."

"Yes. That is a long story!"

"Well, these stories will all be told. It will be a great Sun Dance."

The young man kicked his horse forward, on along the line, looking for someone to visit.

Yes, thought Wolf, *there will be some momentous happenings.*

23

»»»

The Mountain band arrived the following day, with a repetition of the mock charge and the excitement of renewed patriotism. Wolf, White Feathers, and Fast Turtle took part in the exuberance, riding and yelling with the rest. There were even some of the young men from the outsiders who joined in at the invitation of Fast Turtle. It was an exciting and joyous occasion, a mixture of carnival, religious celebration, and repatriation. For the People, this was the biggest and most important event of the year.

There would be quite some time involved, Singing Wolf realized now. The Eastern band had not yet arrived. Even after they did, it would be several days before the ceremonies actually started. There must be the announcement, carried out by the keeper of the Sacred Bundle. For three days this holy man would circle the camp with his apprentice, chanting the announcement. Then the ceremonies themselves would last five more days.

That was good, and it gave opportunity for everyone to dance and pray and make appropriate sacrifices to fulfill vows. For Wolf, it was a long time, because during any of these days . . . or nights . . . White Feathers might spend his time in courting. Wolf had changed his attitude somewhat and was more comfortable with himself. The crises that the two had shared had drawn them closer. They were still rivals, but friends. It was no longer a subject that could not be discussed, their contested courtship. The hatred that Wolf had once felt was now gone.

His awareness of the threat was not. Again it became apparent that time spent with his rival could not be spent by White Feathers in courting. Unfortunately, it could not be used in courting by Wolf, either. But that did not bother him. He had come to think that time was on his side. If he could prevent his rival's courtship from coming to its logical end, then White Feathers—and Rain—might tire of it. And he, Wolf, had many years of friendship and good memories in his favor. In short, if he could prevent any decision on Rain's part, maybe Rain's anger would cool. She would come to her senses and realize that her lifelong dream lay with him, not with the handsome stranger.

Still, he dared not push her. That might renew her rage and make her choose the wrong path. His own best course, he had decided, was to keep his rival occupied and do nothing to anger Rain in the meantime. That would allow him to play for time. There were plenty of distractions that he could use to his advantage, with the events surrounding the Sun Dance.

With all this in mind, he did all he could to occupy White Feathers' time. It was actually not too difficult. There were races and contests, and wagering on both. A couple of times he asked White Feathers to accompany him and Turtle on a short hunt. He praised his rival's horse and asked for a demonstration of its effectiveness. They visited the other bands and asked for tales of the events of their year.

If all else failed, Wolf had one more trick. He would ask for White Feathers' help with his thunderstick. It was better, even, than asking about his horse. No man is able to refuse a request for advice about weapons. They could spend an entire afternoon loading, shooting, and discussing the fine points of the thunderstick's use and care. He was saving that trick for an emergency.

It appeared that he might need it, because White Feathers was growing restless, and there was no sign yet of the Eastern band. The announcement could not begin until they arrived. Wolf felt that Rain, too, was becoming restless. Maybe she had figured out his strategy and, if so, she would surely resent it. Something must happen soon.

Fortunately, something did happen. The wolves reported the approach of the Eastern band. There was a general rush on the part of the young men to grab their horses and ride out for the mock attack in greeting.

For an instant, it seemed that there was a hesitation on the part of White Feathers. Before Wolf could even wonder about it, however, White Feathers was swinging to the saddle.

"Come on," he called. "I want you to meet my parents!"

He struck heels to his horse, and Wolf and Turtle hurried to overtake him. *It is good,* thought Wolf; *this will limit him a little bit.* Wolf had feared for a moment that White Feathers intended to stay at the camp to finalize the courtship that would lead to marriage. He had no way of knowing how close to an understanding White Feathers and Rain had come. Not close, he hoped.

Another thought struck him. Was White Feathers hurrying to tell his parents of his coming marriage? All this uncertainty was difficult.

The riders topped a low rise and, there in the valley below, could see the Eastern band. The column straggled across the prairie for some distance, a disorganized collection of straggling travelers.

"Aiee!" exclaimed Fast Turtle. "Look at them. Three days late and just moping along!"

White Feathers gave him an irritated glance, acknowledging the thinly veiled jibe at the Eastern band.

Then the riders swept down the slope, to be met by riders from the straggling column.

"Ho, White Feathers!" a young man shouted. "How goes it? We have missed you!"

White Feathers waved in return, and his answer was lost in the swirling mass of horses and riders as the two groups met. Wolf found himself carried along, turning to the left with the thundering charge, riding in a circle that enclosed the entire caravan. Older people on foot or riding the steady old horses that pulled the pole-drags waved in greeting. Children watched in excited awe, dogs ran and barked. The last band had arrived and the preliminary ceremonies of the Sun Dance could now begin.

Wolf was trying to keep up with White Feathers, who was being jostled and greeted by a great many friends. He must be a very popular young man in his own band. Feathers had indicated that he wanted Wolf to meet his parents, but so far it seemed impractical. They had circled the caravan twice, and Wolf's horse was breathing hard. He began to draw out of the frantic melee, trying to slow a little to spare his mount. He saw that others were doing the same. White Feathers, just ahead, now began to pull aside, too, and Wolf fell in beside him. It would be good to walk their horses to cool them out. Fast Turtle was nowhere to be seen, lost in the crowd. He would turn up later.

White Feathers laughed. *"Aiee,* what a ride!"

"Yes. I was starting to worry about my horse," Wolf agreed, patting the animal's sweat-soaked neck.

"It is good to see my friends and relatives," Feathers said happily. "Let us walk the horses out and then we will find my family."

The circling horsemen were slowing now, dropping out to join families and friends, or simply continuing to walk as they talked excitedly about their experiences since they last met.

A horse pushed up alongside White Feathers on the other side, and Wolf saw that the rider was a young woman. Hardly more than a girl, actually, but one of the most beautiful that Wolf had ever seen. He tried not to stare, but it was difficult. Her large, deep-set eyes were soft and feminine, her smile mischievous. Her long body seemed athletic in its graceful rhythms, the shapely legs exciting as they gripped the ribs of the gray mare.

"*Ah-koh,* White Feathers! You came back. It is good. I promised to wait for you!"

Wolf was astonished, but apparently no less than was White Feathers.

"Do I . . . Who . . . Gray Bird?" he gasped.

The girl laughed.

"Yes, Feathers. Gray Bird, the little girl, your friend's sister."

Wolf's eyes swept over her. This young woman would be tall as well as shapely, he saw. Certainly no "little girl."

"*Aiee,* you grew up!" blurted White Feathers.

She laughed again, a lovely lighthearted sound, one to turn any man's heart.

"Yes," she said proudly. "You were gone a long time. A whole season. But I told you to wait for me. I grew up for you!"

White Feathers seemed to have forgotten Wolf. In fact, he seemed to have forgotten nearly everything. He was completely occupied in staring at the beautiful creature on the gray mare.

"But . . ." he stammered, trying to regain his composure, "you did not tell me it would be like this!"

"You approve, then?" she teased.

"I . . . Of course!"

"It is good!" She looked flirtatiously at Singing Wolf, her eyes inviting. "And now, who is your handsome friend?" she asked.

Wolf knew that the flirtation was only to impress White Feathers, but his heart melted anyway. *Aiee! Handsome, she had said!* How good it felt, such a remark from such a desirable woman!

White Feathers turned and looked at Wolf as if he had never seen him before. Then an amused expression crossed his face.

"This one?" he asked, mischief in his eyes. "I do not know. He is a stranger to me!"

Now all three laughed.

"I am Singing Wolf, of the Southern band," he told her. "This tongue-tied one is my friend, too. You are Gray Bird?"

"Yes . . . I will see you both later!"

She put heels to her horse and loped ahead, leaving both men staring after her.

"She was only a little girl," mumbled White Feathers in confusion.

Wolf laughed.

"But she grew up, my friend."

"Yes," Feathers agreed. "She surely did!"

24
>> >> >>

The world had suddenly changed for Singing Wolf. In truth, he now felt like singing. White Feathers was obviously smitten by the appearance of a childhood friend, now grown into a woman. An unexpectedly beautiful woman, it seemed, one who was attracting the attention of all the young men as well as that of White Feathers.

It was apparent from the first, however, that Gray Bird fully intended to claim her brother's boyhood friend as her own. She openly said so. It was equally apparent that White Feathers had no thought of resisting. All thought of other courtships had vanished, and the sound of his courting flute was heard only around the camp of the Eastern band.

All of this was good in the eyes and thoughts of Singing

Wolf. The pressure and worry of his need to court Rain were eased, and he could look forward to a reconciliation. He was a little fearful about that, realizing that he must be cautious. Rain would probably be feeling some rejection, even a little anger, maybe, at White Feathers' sudden loss of interest. Wolf knew the feeling of rejection all too well. Yes, he would first reestablish the friendship, and when that was comfortable again . . . well, then they could talk.

Even now, the feeling of release from the rivalry was good. His friendship with White Feathers was easier, more natural. He found himself glad for the romance of White Feathers, and not just because it made his own life easier. His heart was good for his friend's happiness. And now, his burden lifted, Wolf found himself ready to enjoy all the excitement of the Sun Dance to the fullest.

The Eastern band had finally arrived, amid the usual jokes about having lost their way. Their camp was quickly established in their traditional segment of the circle, just to the north of Sun Boy's opening on the east. It had been announced that though the day was late, the Big Council would proceed that very evening. There were important matters to be considered.

Not the least of these was the coming of the strangers, who now camped near the Southern band. Already there had been much curiosity about these newcomers. As darkness gathered, so did the People, around the council fire. The leaders of each band began to take their places in the traditional segment of the circle. These segments corresponded to the place of that band's camping area. The Northern and Southern bands, of course, in their respective directions. The Red Rocks to the southwest,

the Mountain band northwest. Just to the south of the
opening left for Sun Boy was an empty space, reserved for
the Lost Band. This missing group, it was said, had been
exterminated many lifetimes ago, before the People came
south to the Sacred Hills. The exact circumstances were
unknown or forgotten, but their place in the Council had
always been held open in respect. And, of course, in case
any of them ever returned.

The Real-chief opened the Council, and the pipe was
passed, with prayers to the four winds, sky, and earth.
When the circuit was completed, it was time for the
leader of each band to speak, relating the experiences of
the year.

Broken Lance, as chief of the first band to the left of
the Council circle's "doorway," was first to speak. The old
man was still impressive, Wolf had to admit. He told of
their winter, and their general good fortune.

"There are two things that I would bring before the
Council," he went on. "First is the matter of the thundersticks. I would set that aside until all have spoken. This
weapon may become important, as much so as the coming
of the elk-dog, maybe. But I would hear from others on
that. For now, I would speak instead of these strangers
who camp with us. You have met some of them in the past
few days. You have probably also heard that there was a
killing. One of our young men killed a warrior of theirs to
prevent an ambush."

There was a subdued gasp, as some had apparently not
heard that story.

"But now," Broken Lance went on, "I would ask their
chief to tell you of his people, and why they are here."

He turned and signed to the visitor, who rose and began to sign. The man's gestures were simple and eloquent, as he told his story of hardships and pressure from shifting, warlike neighbors. He apologized for the misunderstanding that had caused the death of one of his young men. By the time he finished, his audience was completely attentive.

Broken Lance thanked him and then spoke to the Council. "Would anyone have questions of him?"

There were several.

"What do they want?"

"I am made to think," Broken Lance said slowly, "that their hearts are good. They want only a place to live and hunt. They will move on if we wish."

A brief argument ensued, one faction questioning the wisdom of more people, the other pointing out the advantage of strength in numbers. Finally an old woman asked to speak and was recognized by the Real-chief.

"Is this our Lost Band?" she asked simply.

There was stunned silence at such a suggestion. Everyone seemed to be looking at Broken Lance.

"I think not," the old chief said hesitantly. "They speak a different tongue. But let us ask him."

He relayed the question to the visiting leader, explaining briefly the story of the Lost Band and the gap in the circle.

The visitor chuckled and shook his head.

"We are not lost," he signed. "We are *here*." There was a ripple of laughter, and he continued. "I think not. Our talk is different. Our looks are different. But many of our customs are the same because we use horses and hunt buffalo, as you do."

In the end, his statements were well-received, and the

Council proceeded to other things, with no real decisions on the newcomers or on the matter of thundersticks.

Singing Wolf found that he had regained much of his confidence when he next encountered Rain. Both were a little shy at first, but willing to try.

It was nearing sunset, and the vast beauty of the big prairie sky was at its best now, in the Moon of Roses.

"Sun Boy chooses his paints well tonight," Rain observed.

"Yes . . . Never better."

"Let us walk," she suggested. "That hill . . . ?"

"It is good," answered Wolf.

They strolled to the rise behind the camp and sat, looking at the panorama below. In another day the formal portion of the Sun Dance would begin. The open-sided brush arbor that would provide shade for the dancers was under construction, and the extended family of the Real-chief had sent their young men out to procure the most magnificent buffalo bull available as the basis for the effigy at the altar. Its head and hide would complete the illusion.

Wolf had been thinking long and hard about what he might give in sacrifice as he made his prayers of thanksgiving for the good fortune that had been his. There was no way in which he could have shown his thanks for the return of Rain's friendship. He had very little to give, in fact, except his thunderstick. He had actually considered sacrificing that, so great was his appreciation. With his father's help, he had decided on a vow instead. He would pledge the best of the season's furs, to be given at the next

Sun Dance. This made him feel better, more confident. Now, how could he explain to Rain how he felt about her?

"I have missed you, Wolf," Rain whispered.

"I, too. I should not . . ."

She laid a gentle hand on his lips.

"Shh . . . Be still!" she said. "You talk too much!"

Yes, he thought. That may have been his problem with her. She snuggled closer, and they watched the changing colors in the west as the distant shadows crept across the prairie.

"It is good," he said.

The strangers from the north attached themselves loosely to the Southern band, often camping together and assisting in the great fall hunts. In a generation, they had been accepted to the point that a place in the circle of the Big Council was made for them, between those of the Southern band and the Lost Band. They maintained their own customs and their dignity as a separate group.

The acceptance of the thunderstick was a little more erratic. It required the advent of more trapping to enable trade. Many preferred to spend the cold winter moons in their warm lodges, sharing a pipe with friends. So, for a while longer, each did as he saw fit, and it was good.

GENEALOGY

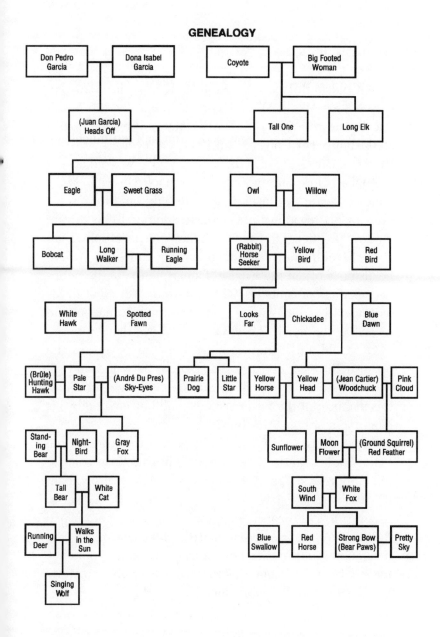

Don Coldsmith was born in Iola, Kansas, in 1926. He served as a World War II combat medic in the South Pacific and returned to his native state, where he graduated from Baker University in 1949 and received his M.D. from the University of Kansas in 1958. He worked at several jobs before entering medical school: He was YMCA Youth Director, a gunsmith, a taxidermist, and for a short time a Congregational preacher. In addition to his private medical practice, Dr. Coldsmith has been a staff physician at the Health Center of Emporia State University, where he also teaches in the English Department. He discontinued medical pursuits in 1990 to devote more time to his writing. He and his wife of thirty-two years, Edna, operate a small cattle ranch. They have raised five daughters.

Dr. Coldsmith produced the first ten novels in the Spanish Bit Saga in a five-year period; he writes and revises the stories first in his head, then in longhand. From this manuscript the final version is skillfully created by his longtime assistant, Ann Bowman.

Of his decision to create, or re-create, the world of the Plains Indians in the early centuries of European contact, the author says: "There has been very little written about this time period. I wanted also to portray these Native Americans as human beings, rather than as stereotyped 'Indians.' As I have researched the time and place, the indigenous cultures, it's been a truly inspiring experience for me. I am not attempting to tell anyone else's story. My only goal is to tell *a* story and tell it fairly."